Twins

Book 1

Swapped

Katrina Kahler

Table of Contents

PROLOGUE

Ali

The throb of my pulse quickened as I raced up the hill. Something was wrong. I had no idea what, but I felt my anxiety deepen with each step. The crest of the hill was so close yet so far. The muscles in my legs burned. If I stopped, I would probably fall over and not reach the top. I pushed through the uncomfortable cramps in my legs and abruptly stopped at the edge of the steep incline. I leaned over, catching my breath as my worst fears were realized.

The car pulled out of the lot. The girl in the backseat turned her head. She had the exact same profile as me. Where was she going? Why was she leaving? And now what was I supposed to do without her?

CHAPTER ONE

Casey

One week earlier…

I rolled over in bed and blinked a few times until the red numbers on the clock on my bedside table formed. I blinked some more, the numbers not moving. But they didn't make sense. It couldn't be that late—

The animated voice of my brother, Lucas, could be heard from the kitchen down the hall.

I jolted awake. Lucas was never up before me. Normally, Mom had to drag him out of bed. I looked at the clock again, and it all made sense.

Oh my gosh! The time wasn't wrong. I was terribly late!

Jumping out onto the floor, I sprinted down the hall to the kitchen. Lucas had his action figures on the table and was making them stomp all over the cereal box while exaggerated explosion sounds poured from his mouth.

Mom was dressed in a pants suit and her hair was slicked back into a bun. She was pulling out file folders from her bag and placing them on the table. She had a meeting that morning. She always got up early for her meetings, why didn't she bother to wake me?

"It's about time you were up," she said without looking at me.

"Mom! You were supposed to wake me up earlier!"

"That's what an alarm clock is for," she said, continuing to organize the file folders on the table.

I placed my hands on my hips. "I forgot to set it, I was up last night finishing the paper for Miss Halliday's class."

She turned around to look at me, her brown eyes wide and unconcerned. "Well, that will teach you about responsibility."

I ground my teeth together. I wanted to argue more, but I didn't even have enough time for that. Instead, I grumbled loudly enough for her to hear and ran back to my room. I only had ten minutes before the bus was scheduled to arrive. When I looked in my full-length mirror I could have screamed. My hair was a tangled brown mess atop my head, and my eyes were still sleepy. I resembled a zombie. I opened my dresser drawer and pulled out a random outfit for the day. Anything would have to do. I couldn't be late for school. Not after staying up until eleven-thirty the night before finishing off my paper. The paper was half my grade for the semester, and Miss Halliday didn't give excuses for late work.

After dressing, I brushed my teeth and combed my hair. It was a good thing I decided to shower the night before. My hair was something I never had to worry about. It obeyed with the stroke of a brush, smoothing down into glossy waves over my shoulders.

I finished with enough time to grab a granola bar and water. Then I rushed out of the house to the bus stop. Lucas was already there with his dorky friends.

I took a breath as the bus appeared down the road. I'd made it! I smiled and knew that today would be okay.

At least I thought so until a short while later. We were on the last stop before school and I remembered the one thing I'd forgotten. The only thing that mattered all week. I saw the five-page paper in my mind's eye, sitting on my desk where I placed it after I printed it the night before.

No, no, no!

My stomach twisted, and my throat tightened. How

could I forget the most important thing? I'd been so concerned with how I looked that I forgot to put the assignment in my bag. I shoved my fingers through my hair, lifting the tresses from my suddenly hot neck.

Gripping the top of the seat in front of me, I wanted to propel myself down the aisle, off the bus and race home. I'd never make it to school on time, but at least I'd have my paper. Being late would be better than my paper not in Miss Halliday's hands by the end of the day.

"No standing!" Mr. Chambers, the bus driver, shouted at me. His eyes looked at me in the mirror above his head.

A few kids glanced towards me, and I slumped down in my seat. Could this day get any worse?

I used the school's front office phone to call Mom's cell. She didn't pick up so I had to leave a message.

"Mom, I forgot my paper on my desk. It's crucial for my grade. Please drop it by the school office after you get this…" I trailed off then hung up. I knew she wouldn't leave whatever meeting she had, once she got to work. Her job was so important to her, more than her daughter. Why did Mom wake Lucas and not me? Our bedrooms were right next to each other. Once again I was an afterthought. Now I had to go to class without my paper and probably get a stern lecture from Miss Halliday and a failing grade.

A tear slipped from my eye, and I wiped it away. I glanced at the clock, realizing I only had two minutes to get to class.

I thanked the secretary for letting me use the phone

and tried to ignore the pitying look on her face.

The final bell rang when I reached the top of the stairs. I ran down the hallway and arrived at the classroom too late. The door was closed, and all of my classmates were looking at the front of the room. I placed my hand on the knob and slowly turned it, trying not to make a peep. I expected all eyes to be on me, but this was not the case. Everyone listened with rapt attention as Miss Halliday spoke. She moved, and I saw a girl next to her at the front of the room.

I gasped lightly and wondered if I were still dreaming, the girl in front of the classroom looked exactly like me. I pinched my arm and bit down on my lip from the pain. I was definitely awake. I looked down at my clothes and realized we were wearing different outfits. Maybe I was still sleepy and seeing things. There were plenty of brown-haired girls in the world, she was just another one.

"Take a seat, Casey," Miss Halliday said with a smile, showing a smear of lipstick on her front teeth. "Class, I want to introduce our newest transfer student."

I found my seat and dropped my bag next to it before sitting. Whenever anyone was late for class, Miss Halliday always made an example out of them. I supposed I had the new girl to thank.

"OMG!" my best friend, Brianna, Brie for short, whispered in my ear. "She looks just like you!"

Brie sat in the seat behind me, and I waved her off. "No, she doesn't."

Though I knew deep down, I was only fooling myself. I looked at the new girl again, and I felt as if I were looking into a mirror. The only differences being her long braid cascading down her back and her shy expression. Her pretty top complemented her dark eyes and olive complexion. The same color eyes and complexion that strangers complimented me on all the time.

I pinched myself again to be certain I wasn't dreaming.

"This is Ali Jackson," Miss Halliday announced to the class. "I'd like you all to make her feel welcome."

The class chorused, "Hello, Ali."

Her eyes darted around the room, and she gave a small smile and a wave. "Hi, everyone."

I narrowed my eyes, inspecting every detail of the girl, desperate to find more differences. Though with Brie's confirmation of what I saw, I was almost sure that I wouldn't find any. How the heck was this possible?

"You can take the empty chair next to Grace," Miss Halliday said while pointing to the back of the room.

"Thank you." Ali started down my aisle, and I turned my head, allowing my hair to cover my face when she passed.

Miss Halliday went to her desk to take attendance.

A few moments later I glanced behind me. Ali had her hands clasped together on the desk, and just as I turned, she looked in my direction.

Her eyes flicked to mine, and her eyebrows shot up in surprise. She stared at me and I could see that she was as startled as I was.

I whipped around, embarrassed at being caught. Who did this girl think she was anyway? Out of the thousands of schools in the country, she had to come to mine? And look like me nonetheless. This entire day was shaping up to be the worst of my life. I didn't want to fathom what else could go wrong.

"Alright class," Miss Halliday said, brushing her hands over her knit skirt. She didn't have the best fashion sense for, but she was my favorite teacher. I wondered if she would give me a break since I was never late with assignments. With my luck so far that day I doubted it.

"Let's all turn to page fifty-four in your books," she

continued.

I pulled the book out of my bag and placed it on my desk. While going to the appropriate page, I glanced behind me once more.

My cheeks heated up when my crush, Jake Hanley, turned in his seat and offered to share his book with Ali.

She smiled at him and moved closer. He leaned forward to say something to her, but I couldn't quite make out what he said. She covered her mouth and quietly laughed.

Of course she did! He was the cutest boy in our grade! Jake rarely talked to me, and now he was chatting away with someone who looked exactly like me? So unfair!

I whirled around in my seat, fuming. I could imagine their conversation. Her with her flirty eyes—my exact eyes—and him getting to know her instead of him getting to know me. I'd tried all year to get him to notice me, and she walks in here on her first day and catches his attention right away.

Ugh!

While Miss Halliday rambled on about something in the book, I found I couldn't take my eyes away from Jake. Ali was following the text on the page, and he was staring at her. How come he never looked at me that way? It was clear Ali and I looked a lot alike, even though I disliked her for that. Maybe it was because Jake and I had gone to school together since kindergarten that he didn't see me in the same way. The new kids who came into the school were always popular, but soon enough she would be ordinary like the rest of us. I hoped so, anyway!

"Casey," Miss Halliday said.

Ali's eyes met mine again while Jake continued to watch her.

I turned around in my seat to meet Miss Halliday's gaze.

"Pay attention please," she said.

"S-sorry," I said and slunk down in my chair.

Miss Halliday continued with the lesson, and I struggled to concentrate. I wanted to look back again to see if Jake and Ali were getting closer than we ever had, but I didn't want to risk being caught out. Instead, I stared at the clock, counting down the minutes until the next bell.

CHAPTER TWO

Brie and I walked outside together for recess. We put our bags down at the designated spot by the stairs and started for the benches on the far end of the lot. A few kids already were sitting there, but there were enough spots for the two of us. We squished together on the end of the bench just as Ali came outside. The seat was cold and still damp from the night before, the sharp feeling under me added to my annoyance.

My chest tightened as I watched her. She was alone for two seconds before Jake and his friends welcomed her into their group.

"It's so unfair," I said to Brie.

"Tell me about it," she said. "If I didn't know any better I'd say you were sisters. Twins, even."

"Really?" I said and squinted my eyes. From that distance, Ali could be any other girl. But then I remembered seeing her up close where the resemblance was uncanny.

"Yeah, actually," Brie said. "Unbraid her hair and she's basically you. You have the same brown eyes, same nose, same chin..."

"Chin?" I asked, touching my own. I didn't realize it was unique enough to compare to others.

Brie shrugged. "You know what I mean. You have the same facial features and skin tone. It's odd actually."

"Really odd." *Nauseatingly odd.*

Brie turned to me, her leg bumping into mine. "I read this article once that said everyone has a look-alike somewhere in the world. Most of the time they aren't related. Something with genetics or whatever. That's crazy, right? Maybe Ali is your look-a-like."

Across the way, Ali was laughing with Jake and his friends. I silently wished she was across the world, and I'd never discovered her.

"People always say that Adam looks like Daniel Radcliffe."

I turned to her. "Your little brother, Adam?"

"It's so annoying," Brie continued. "People come up to him all the time in the grocery store, the mall, wherever! Now he's starting to believe it. I can't go into any room in the house without finding a wand. And he always insists on wearing my dad's robe which is way too big for him. And to make matters worse, he says he wants to be a famous actor someday."

I laughed. "As a Harry Potter look-a-like?" Letting out my laughter made the tightness in my shoulders loosen.

Brie groaned. "Probably! I can't even watch the movies in the house now without him reciting the entire thing!"

Adam did look like Harry Potter, I had made the assumption before since those books were my ultimate favorites. I'd even said it to Adam a few times, myself. I hated being one of the ones to annoy Brie. I made a mental note to keep those thoughts to myself from now on, even though the likeness was definitely there!

While Brie's attempt to make things better had helped, I still felt uneasy about Ali. I couldn't quite put my finger on it. I'd never felt so strange about a person before. It was as if I had some new supernatural sense, but only about Ali. Besides that, I was the only person in my class with someone who looked like me. It was just weird!

Brie chatted on about something else. I tried to pay attention, but I couldn't think of anything besides Ali. I tried to find some more differences between us as the day wore on but I couldn't. I'd never been more excited for school to be over so I could go home and get the day over with.

I tossed and turned the whole night dreaming that I was being chased by hundreds of look-a-likes. It was terrifying!

For the first time ever, I was happy when my alarm clock went off. I set it for an extra half-hour early so I wouldn't be rushed like I was the day before. Miss Halliday had been in a good mood the previous afternoon and gave me a second chance to hand in the paper that I'd left at home. She said everyone was allowed to have an off-day. And what a day it had been!

I made sure to place the paper in my backpack and leave it by the door so I wouldn't forget. I was ready for school with fifteen minutes to spare. Plopping down on the couch, I flipped on the television, dreading going into school and seeing Ali. My dreams from the night before still haunted me, but there wasn't anything I could do about the new girl. Secretly, I hoped whatever made her move to our town would change and she could leave. Though I doubted that would happen. That would be a miracle indeed!

Lucas bounded into the room, full of energy. I wasn't

sure where he got it all from that early in the morning. As usual, he was wearing his favorite yellow hat. I swore he must even wear it to bed, I never saw him without it on his head.

"How come you're watching T.V. before school?" he asked, scrambling to get his arm into his shirt.

"I got up early."

"Mom!" Lucas called. "Is Casey allowed to watch television?"

I swatted at him, but he jumped back with a goofy grin on his face.

Mom strode into the room, already dressed and perfectly presented for another meeting. Twice in one week wasn't common. She smoothed her hand over her hair and rolled her eyes. "I don't have time for this bickering. Lucas, finish your breakfast."

I smirked at him. At least she didn't tell me I had to turn the television off. Mom's uncaring attitude had finally worked in my favor.

Switching my gaze back to the T.V. my thoughts returned to the new girl at school and my uneasy feelings about the day ahead.

CHAPTER THREE

During gym class, Mr. Pavoni our gym teacher, announced that he was splitting the class into pairs for volleyball and we were to practice bumping the ball to each other. Brie and I moved closer together and I grabbed her arm, hoping Mr. Pavoni would get the hint that we wanted to be partners. He gave us a look but then nodded his head in agreement. Brie and I jumped up and down with excitement. I jogged to the bag of volleyballs and picked one out for us.

Over the past few weeks in class, I'd become really good at volleyball. I wasn't normally the sporty type but volleyball seemed to come naturally to me.

Brie, on the other hand, struggled with the concept of hand-eye coordination. She either missed it entirely or hit the ball over our heads. I was happy to be her partner and help her get better, but I was pretty sure volleyball wasn't her sport. At least she could laugh at her attempts. It helped smooth the knot in my stomach over Ali's presence.

Halfway through class, Mr. Pavoni asked us to switch partners to practice serving.

I immediately looked at Jake. My nerves jumped, and I wondered how cool it would be for Mr. Pavoni to pick me as Jake's partner.

Mr. Pavoni had sorted most of the class before he came to me. "Casey, since you're doing well, how about you help out our new student. And Grace can work with Brie."

My body froze. I looked to my right where Ali stood next to Grace. Grace moved over to Brie's side, and I reluctantly stepped closer to Ali.

Mr. Pavoni was completely oblivious to the fact that Ali and I looked alike. After he finished swapping everyone. He blew his whistle, and everyone started to practice serving.

I handed Ali the ball, and she held it in her hands as if she were handling a foreign object. She gnawed on the inside of her cheek, avoiding my eyes.

"Here," I said, taking the ball from her. "You hold it in the palm of your hand like this and then put your other hand into a fist and swing it back." I showed her each motion.

Her eyebrows furrowed.

Geez, even Brie wasn't this clueless. Why did Mr. Pavoni have to stick me with her? I was happy he noticed my progress with the sport, but I needed to be challenged, not brought down to her level.

"I'll show you," I said taking the ball from her.

Ali dropped her hands to her sides. Did she not realize she was supposed to return my serve?

"Put your hands in front of you in the bumping stance."

She looked even more confused than she already had.

Oh well, she'd learn soon enough.

I walked backward, distancing myself from her.

"Ready?"

I could have sworn I heard her say no, but I served it anyway. Hard.

The ball soared over her head, and she ducked. She actually ducked!

Ali looked behind her as our ball rolled away then she looked back at me, her eyes wide with confusion.

I grumbled. "Go get it!"

She nodded and ran for it. When she finally reached it, she walked slowly back to face me. At this rate, the class would be over before I had another turn.

Ali positioned her hands all wrong and barely hit the ball. It plopped a few feet in front of her and rolled the rest of the way to me. I glanced at the clock, needing for the class to be over so I could get away from this Casey-imposter.

I picked up the ball, twirled it in my hands and served it again.

Once again, the ball soared over her head, and I couldn't help a small smile when she missed it completely and had to go running after it again.

Brie was looking at me, and I smiled towards her. Her smile faded when she watched Ali run after the ball.

I looked over, and my stomach dropped. The ball had rolled right to Jake's feet. He bent over to pick it up and handed it to Ali. Their hands brushed, and my cheeks flushed.

He grinned at her and said something to make her smile.

I had the worst luck!

Ali came back to her spot and tried to serve again. And like before, it bounced a few feet in front of her then rolled to me.

"Oops," she said.

She didn't even seem like she was trying. She was probably one of those girls who pretended to be bad at sports so the boys would help her. I was so not that girl. My anger built up inside me as I pictured her with Jake. I served the ball again and like before she didn't even try to go for it. It flew over her head, and she even let out a girly squeal as the ball zipped by.

A loud whistle made me turn around.

Mr. Pavoni came to my side with a stern expression on his face. "That was too hard, Casey. I'm disappointed that you're not trying to help Ali. I think you should sit on the bleachers for a little while and think about what you've been doing."

"But, Mr.—"

"No buts, go." He pointed to the bleachers, and I shuffled towards them, plopping on the bottom bleacher and crossing my arms, fuming.

Mr. Pavoni had taken Ali over to Jake and his partner, Mark, to join in with them.

I sat up straighter, watching them. They threw Ali the ball so lightly a child could hit it. And she still missed! Though instead of complaining, the guys clapped for her and said she did a good job.

My heart raced in my chest. This wasn't supposed to

happen! I wanted to show off how bad she was at the game to bring her down a notch, not make her get closer to Jake!

Jake had moved to Ali's side and showed her how to hold the ball. She did as he said and nailed her next serve.

Ali jumped up and down, cheering.

I had shown her the exact same way to serve, and she had been hopeless. Why was it different with Jake? Probably because he was gorgeous and she wanted to show-off for him.

I watched them play, and Ali began to get better within a few serves.

I didn't realize Mr. Pavoni had come over until he stood directly in front of me.

"Casey, you can play again now if you want. We're going to practice serving a little more before doing a scrimmage."

I stood up, not wanting to miss out on the practice game.

I beelined it towards Ali while Mr. Pavoni called for Mark to be my partner. My heart sank as Mark jogged awkwardly in my direction, then stood waiting for me to pass the ball, a huge grin on his face.

His glasses slid down his nose, and he had to keep pushing them up. I turned around, picking my ball up from the ground. I didn't want to get in trouble again, so I gave him an easy serve. I didn't need to learn a lesson twice in one class. Besides, I had the practice game to show off my skills to Jake, he would be impressed then, and Ali would be ancient history.

Even with the easy serve, Mark managed to miss each one. And on his wild serves, I had to run after every single ball since they either went over my head or nearly knocked out my other classmates. At least with Ali, I didn't need to move to get the ball.

I was relieved when Mr. Pavoni split the class into teams. I made my way over to Brie but then we were told to count off by twos which meant that she was on the other team. All the twos went to the opposite side of the net. With the luck I was having I wasn't sure why I was surprised. I was sorely disappointed that Ali and Jake were on Brie's team as well.

I looked around at my team which was made up of Mark, his only other friend, Kenneth, and some of the girly-girls in my class. Needless to say, we didn't do very well. I had to carry the whole team, and the only points we got were from my impressive serves. Too bad Jake wasn't watching when I served, he was too preoccupied with Ali. At the end of the game they even high-fived! What I wouldn't give to be her at that moment.

Mr. Pavoni dismissed the class, and we went into the locker rooms to change back into our regular clothes.

Some of the more popular girls attached themselves to Ali so they could talk to her.

I'd never felt so invisible. It wouldn't be as annoying if she looked different to me. I began to think it wasn't my looks that were the problem. Maybe it was my personality.

When I told this to Brie, she reassured me there wasn't anything wrong with my personality.

I knew she was trying to make me feel better, but I couldn't shake the uncomfortable feeling inside of me when I thought of Ali.

When the bell rang for lunch, we all left the locker room in one large group. Brie and I walked in front. I couldn't stand to be in the room with Ali any longer.

My body flushed when I saw Jake outside the locker room, leaning against the wall with one foot propped up against it. He looked like a model straight out of a magazine.

When our eyes met, he gave me a broad smile.

I smiled back, my stomach doing somersaults.

The group of popular girls and Ali went over to Jake. He did a double-take from me to Ali and then shifted that adorable smile to her.

He had mistaken me for Ali!

"Want to sit with us at lunch?" Jake asked Ali.

She agreed, and they all walked away.

My shoulders slumped and suddenly I wasn't too thrilled about eating at all. In fact, all I wanted to do right then was go home.

CHAPTER FOUR

After another restless night of sleep, I woke up early to study for my Math exam. All of the numbers in my textbook mushed together in my vision. I skimmed over the equations, confident that I would do fine. I loved Math and tended to do well on assignments and exams. During breakfast, I allowed my mind to wander to Ali. It was disturbing enough that she had the same face, but that uncomfortable feeling I had about her deep inside still hadn't gone away. Thankfully though, it disappeared during the bus ride as I attempted to review the material for the exam.

But when I entered the classroom, the weird sensation became stronger than ever. Then I spotted Ali and Jake at the back of the room, talking. Jake looked really good, especially his messy dark hair. I shook my head and sat in my seat, turning my back to them, but at the same time, I couldn't help straining to hear their conversation. They were speaking too low to hear anything important, but I cringed every time she giggled. I *so* did not laugh like her.

I was grateful when Miss Halliday started class, and I didn't have to hear their voices chatting together any longer.

I breezed through the exam and felt a warmth inside me. Then I looked around and noticed I was the first to finish. I turned over my paper and smiled smugly. Miss Halliday always encouraged those who finished early to check their work, but I didn't think it was necessary. I knew I had aced the exam.

Glancing over my shoulder, I saw Ali with her neck bent toward her desk, chewing on the eraser part of her pencil. She looked worried, and I knew, this time, she would not come out on top.

When the time was up, Miss Halliday asked us to swap papers with the person to our left. I handed my paper along.

Brie leaned forward, her face close to my shoulder. "I don't think I did that well. How do you think you went?"

"Pretty good I think."

Brie scoffed. "You actually like Math, though."

I smiled at her. "I'm sure you did fine."

"Doubt it," she mumbled and sat back in her seat.

I decided to go over the exam with her later and make sure she did better on the next one. Besides, what were friends for?

"Alright, everyone," Miss Halliday said. "Mark only the incorrect answers on the papers in front of you."

I looked at Holly Steadman's paper and saw that she had different answers to mine.

My fingers tightened over my pencil as that uncomfortable feeling returned to my stomach.

Miss Halliday went over the answers to each question, and I saw that Connor Peters had marked several wrong answers on my sheet. That couldn't be right! Holly only had one wrong answer so far, and I couldn't remember what I'd written down for each.

My mouth went dry, and I had trouble swallowing. I

leaned over in my chair to see how many marks Connor had made on my paper. Why didn't I review my answers? My brain was so distracted by Ali that I was about to fail my first Math exam!

There was nothing I could do about the exam now. I turned to Holly's paper and ground my teeth together, concentrating on grading her paper.

After Miss Halliday had gone through all the answers, she asked that we pass our tests forward. I didn't bother to see my grade. I was too embarrassed.

She flipped through the sheets and picked several from the pile.

I sunk down in my chair, hoping she wouldn't want the people with bad grades to stay after class. I was humiliated enough for getting such terrible marks on a subject I was good at. I didn't need everyone else to know how badly I had done.

"Wow!" Miss Halliday exclaimed. "Apparently, I'm doing my job right, most of you did marvelously."

Except for me. Her comment made me feel even worse.

Miss Halliday held up one paper and waved it. "And we have one person who got all of the answers correct. Great job, Ali!"

Jake whooped and clapped his hands. "Go Ali!"

Since he had so many friends, a couple of other kids applauded too.

I turned in my seat to see Ali beaming. She pretended to be embarrassed, but I knew she was proud.

My chin trembled, and I turned around to face the front of the room. Even though we had the same face, Ali was the clear winner in many aspects. She'd caught the attention of Jake, learned to be great at volleyball in one period, and got high marks in class. She appeared to be the better version of me. And it was only a matter of time before I knew I had to accept that.

On the way to lunch, three people asked if Ali and I were related.

"I swear you could be sisters!" Melissa Friedrich said.

"We're not," I snapped.

Melissa didn't sense my attitude and ran off to introduce herself to Ali.

Ali walked a few feet in front of us. And of course Jake was next to her. I wanted to scream, but on the other hand, I couldn't help watching her interact with *my* classmates. Something about her drew me in. Maybe that's what the other kids were feeling. She was strangely captivating. Annoyingly so.

Ali got into the hot lunch line. I really wanted the chicken tenders, but I didn't want to be near her. Instead, I went toward the sandwich line.

"You're passing on the chicken?" Brie asked, following me.

"Yes."

"You never pass on the chicken," she said.

"I know, but I don't want to be around Ali right now. I swear if one more person tells me we look-alike I'm going to scream."

Brie shifted on her feet. "You don't look that much alike. I mean there are similarities, but she wears her hair *way* different. And her style choices are more preppy while you tend to go for casual."

I knew she was trying to make me feel better, it just wasn't working. If Ali took her hair out of the braid and swapped clothes with me, then she would look exactly like me.

"And I think her teeth are a little crooked…" Brie said, trailing off.

I patted her on the arm. "Thanks."

Brie offered a smile then stepped forward to choose her sandwich, allowing me another stolen second to watch Ali. I didn't want to, but I had to accept that Ali was going to be in all my classes. I promised myself to work harder to prove I was the better look-a-like.

CHAPTER FIVE

Later that afternoon when I arrived home, I looked for my mom. I needed an outsider's opinion on the Ali situation. I'd even snapped a picture of her when we were in the library during study hall so I could have photographic proof for her. She almost caught me, but I managed to hide my phone just in time. That would definitely have been embarrassing.

I went to Mom's office and knocked on the door. There was no answer.

"Mom!" I called, knocking again. I knew she was working, but this was important.

I turned the knob and slowly opened the door, calling for her once more.

Inside the room, she was at her desk talking on the phone, which was why she couldn't hear me.

"Mom?" I asked, firmly. I knew I shouldn't interrupt, but I needed to talk to her.

She held up a finger and continued talking.

After what seemed like hours, she finally turned around. "Hon, when my door's closed, I'm working. You know that."

I stepped into the room. "I know, but I have to talk to you about something."

"And it can't wait?"

I was about to say it couldn't, but I stopped myself. If

Mom knew I just wanted to talk about school drama, she'd become annoyed with me for disturbing her important work. And I needed her on my side. "I guess it can wait."

"Well, you've already interrupted me," she sighed. "Tell me the problem."

She continued to type while I quickly told her about Ali and how we look alike and how weird it is at school. I was midway through talking about the Math exam when I realized she was barely paying attention.

I stopped speaking, and she turned around to face me a few moments later. "It doesn't matter if you look similar. It's what's on the inside that counts. Work hard and be the best you can be. I'm sure this girl has flaws too."

"We don't just look *similar*," I said, but she had already turned her attention back to the computer screen. Thinking how quickly she'd shrugged off the conversation, I wondered if I was reading too much into it.

"Is there anything else?" she asked with a slight edge to her voice.

"No," I said dejectedly and started for the door.

"Oh by the way," Mom said. "I'm going away tomorrow for a work trip. Grandma Ann will be watching you."

"You're leaving tomorrow?" I couldn't believe it. She could at least have warned us in advance.

It wasn't the first time she'd done this to us. In fact, she'd gone on more trips this year than we'd ever been on as a family, ever.

"It was a last minute trip, hon. Money is tight now

and with these trips I have the opportunity to bring in a lot more revenue."

"Aren't these trips *costing* money?"

"They are tax-deductible."

I didn't know anything about taxes except that Mom had to deal with them at the beginning of every year. From what I understood is that she had to shell out the money first before seeing any benefits.

From her pinched expression, I knew not to push her further. She was the parent, though most of the time I felt I took over that role. Especially when Grandma Ann was "in charge". I knew I'd be taking care of Lucas who was a handful on regular days. Grandma Ann let him do whatever he wanted, which usually meant that I was left to clean up the mess before Mom returned home.

"Listen, why don't you and Grandma Ann go shopping tomorrow while Lucas is at school?"

I raised an eyebrow. "Skip school to go shopping?" That wasn't something I'd ever imagine Mom saying.

Mom smiled. "It will be fun. Give you two a chance for some alone time."

"But *we* were supposed to do that, remember? I need stuff for school camp next week."

"Casey, please. You're being very difficult. I have to run this household, and we need money to do that. I'm going on the trip, it's up to you if you want to go shopping."

I frowned. As much as I preferred to go shopping with Mom, I could use a break from school for a day to clear my head about Ali. And I did have a growing list of things to get for the school camp trip the following week. It wasn't the most ideal situation but the need to be away from Ali had won.

"Okay," I said.

"Grandma Ann will help you get everything you need, hon. I'm sorry I can't go with you. And think of the bright side, you only have a few days here until your trip. I promise it will go by in a flash."

I seriously doubted that. "I'll let you get back to work."

I left the room and headed for the kitchen. I grabbed a box of cookies from the cabinet and selected a few to take with me to my bedroom. Lucas would be home at any minute and would probably destroy something on the way. I went to my room and closed the door, then sat down on my bed and ate the cookies. The chocolate melted in my mouth, and I began to relax. At least if I was taking the following day off, I didn't have to rush through all my homework. That idea quickly disappeared. I'd have to try double as hard on my homework to make sure each answer was correct. I didn't want a repeat of the Math exam.

Sighing, I opened my backpack, tossing my books beside me. I organized them by subject and started with my English assignment.

Thoughts of Ali filtered through my head, but I was able to push them away for the time being. As the next day was Friday, I wouldn't have to see her until the following week, and I wasn't going to have annoying thoughts of her ruin my day off. Maybe when I returned to school, it would all be better.

I could only hope.

CHAPTER SIX

As much as I dreaded spending the entire day alone with Grandma Ann, it turned out to be the best day I'd had in a while. And the idea of taking the day off school made it so much more fun! Grandma Ann was not normally very generous when it came to spending money, but she wanted to spoil me. So in addition to getting all the essentials for camp, she even bought me a new outfit for Ronnie's birthday sleepover on the weekend.

That night, after the delicious home-cooked lasagna that Grandma Ann made for our dinner, I tried on my new clothes. The black and white top with capped sleeves perfectly matched the white flared skirt. I pulled my black converse high tops from my closet, and they completed the outfit. I couldn't wait to hear all the compliments from the girls! As I twirled around my room I became more and more excited for the party. I could hardly wait.

The following night, Grandma Ann dropped me off at the party. I jumped out of the car and smoothed down my top and skirt wanting to look flawless. I said goodbye to her and headed down the drive towards the front door.

Ronnie opened the door to welcome me, and wrapped me in a hug. "Thanks so much for coming, Casey!"

I handed her a glittering gift box containing a pretty charm bracelet that I'd bought a few weeks earlier. I knew she was going to love it. "Happy Birthday, Ronnie!"

"Thanks, Casey," she beamed at me while at the same time taking in my outfit. "Oh my goodness! I love what you're wearing!"

"Thanks!" I said, smiling back at her. "And I love your denim skirt, Ronnie. It looks so good on you!"

Smiling in return, Ronnie beckoned me to follow her. "Come inside," she said, pointing to the living room. "A few people are here already."

We entered the living room, and I could see that Brie had already arrived as well. She jumped up and came to my side. "Is that your new outfit? It looks awesome on you!"

I'd called her the night before to talk about my shopping trip with Grandma Ann. She seemed just as excited as I was.

I waved to Lacey Gordon who sat on the couch. But then I froze when I realized Ali was sitting next to her. She smiled at me but I turned away in shock, quickly grabbing Brie and dragging her from the room.

"Brie, can show me where to put my bag?" I asked loudly enough for the others to hear. I had to get out of that room.

Brie took me to Ronnie's bedroom and I dropped my bag near the other girl's brightly colored overnight bags.

Then, whirling on her, I could not contain myself any longer, "What is Ali doing here? She just started school, and she's already invited to a sleepover?"

Brie sighed and avoided my eyes. "Well, yesterday in class we had to do a group project. And since you weren't there, Miss Halliday asked Ali to join our team. She's actually really nice, and we ended up hanging out during recess and lunch. When Emily Masters told Ronnie she couldn't make the party, Ronnie invited Ali to come instead. And she accepted."

I crossed my arms, my neck burning with heat. Even when I wasn't in school, Ali was ruining my life. "I can't believe this!"

"I didn't want to tell you because I knew you'd be upset. And I was worried that you might not even come, so I decided not to mention it."

I frowned back at her, clearly unhappy.

"I know it's weird that she looks like you, but seriously, Casey, I think you should give her a chance. I really think you'd get along with her."

That was the last thing I wanted to do and Brie could obviously see from my expression, exactly how I felt.

Chewing on her lip, she shrugged her shoulders, not really sure what else to say. "I guess, we should probably head back in there, Casey. They'll be wondering where we are."

"Yeah," I said reluctantly, as I followed her back to the living room.

After finding a spot on the couch next to Ronnie, I tried to put on a happy face, though it was hard, especially with Ali in the room. I glanced at her every so often. She had merged into the group so easily and after only one day of my absence! She looked so good in what she was wearing. Her outfit was so cool.

It took me a minute, and then I recognized the top she

had on. I'd seen it the day before at one of the boutique shops at the mall. It was the exact one I would have loved to wear but when I saw the price tag through the window, I felt bad asking Grandma Ann to buy it as it was so overpriced. I'd been thinking about it ever since and seeing it on Ali proved how nice it would have looked on me.

Ali's family must have a lot of money to afford that top. I added that to the list of things I didn't like about her. If only I hadn't been selfish and gone shopping with Grandma Ann, I could have been in the class group instead of Ali and she would never have been invited. It would have cost me my new outfit but at that point, I didn't care.

Just then the doorbell rang, and Ronnie got up from the couch to answer it. It gave me another opportunity to watch Ali unnoticed. She had turned to face Lacey, and they were chatting away about something. What could they possibly have in common? Lacey was always the girl that I had trouble getting to know as she was so shy, but somehow Ali had managed to befriend her in only a few days.

When all the guests arrived, Ronnie suggested we play some games while we waited for the pizza to be delivered. Placing a few sheets of paper on a nearby table, she explained, "Here are the lists for the scavenger hunt. The first team to find everything will win a prize! And it's a good one too," Ronnie said, grinning widely.

I moved to Brie's side so we could be on the same team.

"I want to be on Ali's team!" Lacey said, jumping up from the floor and moving to stand by her.

"Me too!" Ronnie said, folding her arms adamantly. "I'm the birthday girl, so I get dibs!"

Holly was visibly disappointed that she couldn't be on Ali's team.

"Holly, we can be on the same team for the next game," Ali reassured the girl.

My hands clenched into fists. I felt as if the world had flipped on its side. Sure, Brie and I were always on the same team, but no one had ever fought to be on my team before. And here was Ali, the new girl who fit in better than I did.

My shoulders slumped. What I thought would be a fun night had quickly turned into a disaster, and it was all Ali's fault!

Just to add to my frustration, Ali, Ronnie, and Lacey's team won the scavenger hunt. They even made up a fun dance to celebrate. Holly and Brie wanted to learn the dance too. They both gathered around Ali who was teaching them the moves.

I was not in a dancing mood. Instead, I sat on the couch with my arms crossed.

"Why aren't you dancing with us?" Holly asked with an encouraging grin.

Each of the girls looked at me, and I felt embarrassed. I stood up and mustered a smile while I attempted to copy the moves. All of their attention returned to Ali.

"What's the next game?" I asked Ronnie a few minutes later.

She was too busy with Ali to hear me. I nibbled on my lip and moved away from the group, needing a second to myself. This time, no one seemed to notice my absence. Heat prickled behind my eyes, but I was determined not to cry.

Later in the evening, after games, pizza, cake and ice cream, we set up our sleeping bags in the living room on top of mattresses. I made sure I was on the edge next to Brie, so I could be as far from Ali as possible. I wanted to go to sleep and then go home so I could enjoy what was left of my Ali-free weekend.

I grabbed my toothbrush and headed for the bathroom. The door was ajar so I pushed through and came face-to-face with Ali.

"Oh, sorry," I said, turning away. "I didn't think anyone was in here."

"You can stay. There's plenty of room," she said.

I hesitated. It would be weird if I left after she'd said that. But I really didn't want to be alone with her. In the end, I decided to stay.

Ali moved away from the sink and slid her toiletry bag closer to her, making room for mine.

I put it down and dug through it for my toothbrush and paste. I smeared the paste on the toothbrush and brushed my teeth as quickly as I could.

"This party is so much fun," Ali said.

"Mmhmm," I said, still brushing.

"I've never been to a sleepover birthday before. It's a cool idea."

I nodded and continued to brush.

"Everyone has been so kind to me this week. It made the change to your school so much easier."

"That's good," I said and rinsed the foamy toothpaste

from my mouth.

Ali smiled and pulled the elastic from her braid, working her fingers through her hair.

I watched as the only big difference in our looks faded into oblivion. She brushed her long locks into soft waves over her shoulders. The exact same way I always wore my hair!

We stared at each other through the mirror for a few seconds before Ali looked away. She continued to brush her hair while I finished up. The effect was striking and this time, I found it hard not to gape at the girl. We really did look like the same person. The effect was even more so with her change in hair style. Her brown eyes followed the strokes of the brush, up and down, up and down.

I fiddled in my bag for something, not wanting to leave yet. I just had to know.

I turned to her at the same time as she turned to me. "Why do you have my face?" we asked simultaneously.

CHAPTER SEVEN

Ali

Our words hung in the air between us. We looked in the mirror again, and then back at each other. "You look just like me," we said at the same time.

How was this happening? I still couldn't believe that I'd moved to a new school where this girl, Casey, looked exactly like me. And now we were speaking the same words at the same time. Talk about freaky!

Casey's mouth tugged down into a frown, and I felt my lips doing the same. I looked in the mirror at her. Was she as confused as I was? We had the same facial expression so I guessed she was. I didn't know what to say. My hands had the urge to do something so I picked up my brush again and started pulling it through my hair. I hoped Casey would leave, but at the same time I wanted to know more about why she looked like me.

I moved my hair to the other shoulder and started brushing that side.

"What is that?" Casey asked.

"What is what?" I asked.

"That." She pointed at my shoulder.

I placed my hand over the blemish on my shoulder. "It's a birthmark."

Casey looked at me strangely.

I chuckled lightly. "When I was a kid, I used to try and scrub it off each time I took a bath. Even though my mom told me it was permanent, I always thought it was dirt under my skin."

Casey still said nothing.

My body flushed with embarrassment. I was always protective of that spot and typically wouldn't have shown it, but I felt comfortable about sharing it with Casey for some reason. "I don't mind it now. I think it looks like a heart. Sort of like a tattoo, you know?"

"Yeah," Casey said. "I have a birthmark too." She lifted one leg of her pants and revealed a circular birthmark on her left ankle.

"Birthmarks are common," I said. I was slightly relieved that she didn't have a matching heart-shaped birthmark on her shoulder. That would have taken our same looks to a whole other level.

"When you first came to school," Casey started, "I thought it was really strange how we looked so similar. Brie told me she'd heard that everyone has a look-alike somewhere in the world. I wonder how many people actually get to meet their look-a-like."

"Probably not many."

"It's a freaky coincidence that we're at the same school."

"Totally."

We laughed. I thought it was more lucky than freaky that we did end up meeting. Most people would go through their lives not meeting their look-a-like. It was a very cool idea and even though we weren't close, I liked being around Casey.

"Where are you from originally?" Casey asked.

"I was born in Springfield, Missouri."

She nodded. "How come you moved?"

I winced. It was the question everyone wanted to know. And the one I most feared to answer. I told everyone who asked that it was for my mom's job. That was only part of the truth. The move had been for my mom, but not for a job. For her life. Casey's ability to put me at ease made me feel comfortable opening up to her completely.

"I don't tell a lot of people this," I said. "But my mom is very sick with cancer."

"Oh no, I'm so sorry," Casey said, her eyes filling with concern.

"Thanks." I hesitated a moment before continuing. "We had to move here for her to get the best treatment possible. She's in a trial for a new medicine, and it's our last hope."

"Ali, that's awful," Casey said, touching my arm.

Her touch made me feel as if a weight had been lifted from my shoulders. It felt good to talk to someone about what was going on in my life. The move was scary for many reasons, but on the top of the list was Mom's health.

Tears welled in my eyes. "I don't know what we're going to do without her. It would just be my dad and me. I can't imagine her dying. She's like my best friend." My voice cracked, and tears burst from my eyes.

Casey pulled me into a hug, and I cried into her shoulder. "Ali," she said. "It will be okay. I have no idea what you must be going through, but I know it must be terrible. I'd feel the same way if it were my mom."

A sharp knock at the door made us both jump. Ronnie poked her head through the opening.

"Hurry up you two, we're going to start the movie now. You don't want to miss the beginning."

"We'll be out in a minute," Casey said.

I turned my head to the side to make sure Ronnie didn't see that I was upset. I didn't want to answer any questions about why I was crying.

"Okay, be quick!" Ronnie replied, as she headed back to the living room.

Casey took my hands in hers. "It's going to be okay. You can talk to me anytime about this."

I nodded in response, a feeling of relief flooding through me.

"Now," she continued. "Let's go out there and try to have fun. Forget about all your worries for one night and enjoy the party."

I swallowed and nodded, wiping the streaks of tears from my cheeks. Following along behind her, I had the overwhelming feeling that somewhere we we'd been destined to meet.

CHAPTER EIGHT

Casey

Ali and I entered the room where we could see all the girls splayed out comfortably on the floor ready to watch the movie. The opening credits to the film were playing on the television screen.

"Whoa," Lacey said, staring towards us.

Every pair of eyes turned in our direction.

I looked at Ali then back to the girls, each of them now staring openly. "What?"

Holly's mouth gaped open. "Did you two do this on purpose?"

Ali shrugged. "Do what?"

Brie chimed in. "This is freaky. You two looked similar before but now with Ali's hair down and wearing almost the same color pink pajamas, you could be identical twins!"

Ali smiled at me, and I smiled back. She was so much nicer than I'd initially thought and it felt great that she'd confided in me, trusting me enough with her secret. She was going through a lot with her mom so I couldn't fault her for trying to make new friends, especially at a new school. She was braver than me. I would have been devastated if my mom was sick like hers. She hid it well, but I knew deep down she was hurting. I made a promise to myself to take it easy on her from now on.

"It's starting!" Ronnie exclaimed.

All of the girls settled into their sleeping bags to watch the movie.

Ali headed to her spot across the room. I watched her go, and didn't sit down until she did.

Brie nudged me after I settled in my spot alongside her. "I see you two are getting along now?"

"Yeah," I said. "She's not so bad."

"I told you. It's kinda cool you two look the same *and* are friends."

"Yeah, it is." Until Brie said it, I didn't believe we were friends, but friends told each other secrets. And Ali had chosen to share a big one with me.

The others, including Ali, were fully immersed in the movie. While I usually loved watching fantasy films, I couldn't help thinking about the exchange between Ali and myself in the bathroom. As quickly as my life had shifted when she arrived at school, another change seemed to have taken place the moment she shared her innermost secrets with me. And the fact that we seemed to speak the same thoughts at the same time made my skin prickle.

I struggled to pay attention to the movie but continued to find myself distracted by Ali and our likeness in appearance.

I was relieved when the movie finally ended and everyone began chatting. At last, I could escape my thoughts for a little while.

"That was so good! I can't wait for the sequel," Brie said to the group.

"And how hot is the guy who plays David?" Holly said.

Holly and Ronnie pretended to swoon, falling back on their mattresses. All of the girls giggled at their play-acting.

"It was alright," Ali said. "I don't think any book-to-movie series can compare with Harry Potter."

I sucked in a breath.

"No way!" Lacey said. "Harry Potter is too violent. I love the romance in this series."

Holly and Ronnie agreed with Lacey.

I met Ali's eyes for a brief moment before I spoke. "Ali is right. Nothing compares with Harry Potter."

"I wouldn't argue with her," Brie said, warning the group. "Casey is a serious hardcore Harry Potter fan."

"Well I'm the birthday girl, so I win this conversation!" Ronnie said with a grin.

Then everyone began chatting about their favorite parts of the movie we'd just watched. I listened to the conversation since I hadn't paid much attention to the movie itself. My brain had been too preoccupied with thoughts of my lookalike.

Lacey grabbed her phone. "Who wrote the books? I want to read them since the movies are so good."

The name of the author popped into my head, even

though I hadn't read the books either.

"H.W. Knowles," I said at the exact same time that Ali did.

Everyone looked at Ali and me.

"That was really weird!" Ronnie said.

"Yeah," Brie agreed. "You two look alike, like the same things, and say the same things at the same time. Very freaky!"

"Are you sure you're not twins?" Holly grinned. "That would actually make a lot of sense."

Holly stared at us for a moment longer, waiting for an answer.

I grinned and waved my hand dismissively. I didn't want to entertain the idea of us being twins. It was impossible. I grew up with my mom and Lucas, while Ali was across the country with her parents. That was that.

"I can't hold it in any longer!" Ali declared, a curious expression on her face.

Her outburst made me jump. "Hold what in?" I asked.

She hesitated and looked me straight in the eyes. "I think there might be a possibility we're twins since...I'm adopted."

All of the girls, including me, gasped at the news.

Then the room exploded in noise. Everyone began to talk at once.

Brie grabbed my shoulders. "Oh my goodness!

Imagine you *are* twins and you were separated at birth. It sounds like a movie plot. A really juicy one. Can you imagine that you were adopted by your mom, and no one ever told you?"

I couldn't imagine it. I didn't want to. As much as my mother wasn't around too much, she was my mom. I'd hate it if I found out she'd lied to me all these years. But I really wanted to know more from Ali about her adoption.

Ronnie's mom came into the room. She was in an oversized t-shirt and sweatpants. I'd never seen her without makeup before. She looked as if we'd woken her up. "What is all this racket? It's getting late, time for bed girls."

Ronnie stood up, her eyes wide. "Fifteen more minutes, please Mom?"

Ronnie's mom sighed. "Fifteen minutes then lights out. Don't make me come back out here."

Ronnie shooed her mom out of the room then sat back down on her sleeping bag. "Ali, spill."

Ali's shoulders were tucked under her ears, the attention from all the girls overwhelming. I could almost feel her reluctance to share her story, but there was obviously no turning back now.

"Well," she started. "My parents told me when I was younger that I was adopted. But they never shared anything about my birth mother."

"Did you ask?" Brie questioned.

Ali nodded. "Many times. I love my parents, but I wanted to know more about my real mother; what she was like, and who she was and all that."

"And your parents didn't tell you?" Lacey asked.

Ali sighed. "All they said was that my mom was very young when she had me and she didn't have enough money to take care of a baby. That's pretty much it."

"I would push my mom to tell me everything," Ronnie interrupted.

"It seems to upset her when I ask," Ali said sadly.

I didn't know how long Ali's mother had been sick for, but I could imagine how upsetting it would be for her if Ali continued asking about her real mother. I didn't voice my thoughts since it wasn't my place to tell everyone about her mom's health.

"Did your parents ever tell you where you came from?" Brie asked.

Ali shook her head. "No. I don't think they want me to know too much about it."

"There's something fishy about this situation," Brie said.

I could see her mind ticking over as she contemplated all the details. "Ali?" She asked, "When is your birthday?"

"Tenth of October," Ali replied, her eyes darting towards me.

"OMG!" Brie exclaimed. "The same day as Casey's! That has to be more than coincidence!"

Brie pushing for answers made me feel a little uncomfortable, and I just wished she would stop. Although finding out that Ali and I shared the same birth date was freakier than ever.

"That's it! I agree with Brie," Holly said. "I think you are twins, and someone has been lying."

They all looked at me for confirmation.

"My mom didn't give birth to twins," I said. "It's not possible."

"How do you know?" Brie asked.

"Because I do!" I stated firmly, my cheeks flushing red-hot. "I think we need to get off this topic and go to bed before we get into trouble." I shoved my body into my sleeping bag and turned away from everyone. Mom would never have lied to me about having a twin sister.

The other girls settled down, but not before casting their vote for how they felt about the situation. Then someone turned off the light.

As I drifted off to sleep, a final question floated through my mind. Could Mom have lied to me all these years?

CHAPTER NINE

My obsession with Ali over the last week had switched to obsessing about the theory that we actually *were* twins. The girl's voices from the previous night bounced around my brain making me toss and turn all night. I ended up pushing my mattress further into the hallway the second time Brie kicked me and told me to stop moving around.

I was exhausted the next morning and for once I was happy that Ali was more popular than me. During breakfast, the girls wanted to hear more about her past, and their attention was on her instead of me. I wondered if my sleepy expression told them I wasn't willing to talk about it again.

The one detail that lined up with Ali's adoption was the fact that her real mother had given birth to her when she was very young. If anyone cared to do the math, they would know that my mom had given birth to me at a young age too. But I couldn't even fathom that Ali and I were twins. That would mean Mom had lied to me for years, and I had a sister I didn't even know about!

I shook away the thoughts and decided to prove this theory was wrong. I just wasn't sure how to go about it.

On the way home from Ronnie's, Grandma Ann asked me how the sleepover went.

"It was all right," I said. "We played games and watched a movie."

“That sounds fun!” she said.

“Or booooring,” Lucas said from the backseat.

I whipped around and glared at him. He stuck his tongue out at me in his usual annoying manner.

I turned back around in a huff choosing to ignore him. I was already tired, I didn’t need him bugging me right then.

While I stared out the window, Grandma Ann asked for more details about the night. I didn't want to be rude, but I wasn't in the mood to talk. I was concentrating on the conversation I would have with my mother when she arrived home.

"Casey?" Grandma Ann asked.

"What?" I asked.

"You seem to be in the clouds today. Are you okay?"

"Yes, I'm fine."

She clicked her tongue a few times. "You don't sound fine.'

I really didn't want to get into the specifics of Ali with her, but I knew her well enough that she wouldn't stop asking until she was satisfied with an answer.

"There's this new girl at school, Ali..." I told her the whole story from the beginning. She was always more attentive than Mom, and I found it easy to tell her everything I'd been feeling about the new girl. I kept Ali's secret about her mother's illness though, as I didn't think Grandma Ann needed to know about that.

I was finishing up my story when we pulled into the driveway. Lucas, who had been engrossed in his electronic game in the back seat, jumped out of the car, impatient to get inside and continue his game. Grandma Ann passed him the keys and we watched him walk up the steps towards the front door.

Without him there to overhear, I decided to continue. "All last night the girls were saying that Ali and I could be twins separated at birth. I don't think that's possible but what other explanation is there?"

Grandma Ann turned off the car and her hands dropped to her lap. She stared ahead as if she were in a trance.

"It's not possible, right?" I asked.

She pressed her lips together still not meeting my eye.

Oh my –

I gasped. "Is it true?"

She snapped out of her trance and turned to me. Her face gave away everything. "Casey…"

My eyes welled with tears, but I wasn't sad, I felt utterly betrayed. I pushed on the door handle and shoved the car door open, throwing it closed behind me with a loud bang. Racing to the house, I disappeared through the open front door and sprinted for Mom's room.

I could clearly hear Grandma Ann's voice calling for me from the driveway. But there was no way I wanted to speak to her any further. Quickly slamming Mom's bedroom door closed, I turned the latch and locked it.

My breathing rasped in my ears, and my eyes darted around the room looking for something…anything that could prove what I already knew.

My gaze fell on Mom's cupboard. She had photo albums in there. I pulled out my baby album and whipped through each plastic page, the quick *thwapping* sound matched the pace of my racing heart.

"Casey!" Grandma Ann's voice came from the other side of the door. The knob jiggled, but she wasn't able to get it open.

"Leave me alone!" I shouted.

I expected her to fight. I expected her to yell for me to get out of my Mom's room, but instead there was silence on the other side. I didn't care what she said or what she did, I needed to find proof. I needed to see the proof with my own eyes.

I heard her feet shuffling down the hall away from the door. Then Lucas started talking animatedly about something, and Grandma Ann responded. I wondered how long it would take before she demanded that I open the door. I had to find something quickly before she returned.

I took a breath and continued through the album. Mom hadn't kept up with it over the past few years, she was too busy with work, I guessed. The photos were of me as a baby during birthdays and vacations. There were pictures of me with Grandma Ann and Lucas when he was a baby. But there were no other babies. No twin babies at all. There was nothing to suggest another baby had even existed! I went through the photos again, slower this time. I squinted at each one, trying to find something, anything, to prove I had a twin. After the third time going through the album, I closed it and shoved it away. It slid under Mom's desk, and I didn't care if it was ever found. It was a book of lies anyhow.

I left the room and decided to go right to the source. I confronted Grandma Ann in the living room, watching a show on TV with Lucas.

"Can I talk to you?" I asked her, my eyes blazing furiously.

Lucas looked over and shushed me. "You know this is my favorite part!"

Grandma Ann stood, her face pale and her mouth slightly open. I'd never seen her so nervous.

I walked down the hallway, organizing my thoughts and went into my bedroom. I sat on the edge of my bed but quickly jumped up and began to pace. It felt as though I had jumping beans under my skin. Was I ready to be told the truth?

Grandma Ann closed the door most of the way. "Casey—"

"So it's true? I have a twin?" I interrupted. Each of the questions I had, burst from my mouth at once. "Is my mom even my real Mom? Am I adopted too? Were we separated at birth for some reason? How come no one ever told me?" With each question, my voice began to crack a little more, until my vision blurred with tears.

"Please," I begged, "I just want the truth!"

Grandma Ann took a breath. "Okay. I will tell you everything. You deserve to know it all."

CHAPTER TEN

"You have to understand, Casey," she said. "Your mother was very young when she fell pregnant. Her boyfriend at the time, your birth father that is, decided to leave as soon as he found out. He said he wasn't ready to be a father, and he just left.

It was obviously not an ideal situation. And when we found out your mom was having twins the situation became even more complicated. Your grandfather and I wanted to see your mother graduate high school and go off to do promising things. We refused to let her get a job. She needed to focus on her studies, and she could not do both. And with your sick grandfather to care for, I was unable to add two babies to the household. The cost of his medical bills plus expenses for two babies was just not a possibility.

We found two separate families to adopt her unborn twins as there were no families willing to take two babies at the same time. But your mother would not have it. She refused to give up both of her children, and in the end she chose to take you home. It was so hard for her to make the decision but she could not see both of you go."

I choked on a sob, unable to hold back my tears any longer. Poor Ali! If my mom had chosen differently, I would have been the one who was adopted, not her.

"Your mother was so stubborn," Grandma Ann continued. "She was little more than a child herself, but I couldn't change her mind. I'm so sorry, Casey. She made me promise not to tell you. She wanted to wait until you were older to tell you the truth, hoping by that stage, you'd be able to cope."

She stared at me, her voice faltering as she spoke. This was clearly not an easy conversation for her to have. "Your mother had plans to find your sister long ago. But then she met your stepfather and then Lucas came along. It was only a year into their marriage before your grandfather passed and your stepfather skipped town."

Grandma Ann's voice was sad and furious at the same time, but she was forced to go on. "Everything fell apart for her, and she needed to focus on work to provide for you two. That's why I moved closer, so I could be around to help. And even though I knew you could handle the truth, to her it was never the right time. But you have to believe she didn't want to keep this from you forever. Neither of us ever expected you would find out on your own."

I rubbed my eyes, taking in everything she'd said. Knowing the truth had only made me feel worse. "So if I didn't find Ali, I might never have been told about my twin? Perhaps not until years from now, if ever at all?"

Grandma Ann avoided my eyes, answering the question without any words.

"Please leave," I murmured. I needed be alone. I couldn't stand to have her near me.

Grandma Ann sighed, stepping toward me. "I think we should…"

"Go!" I shouted, backing away from her.

She jumped, surprised at my outburst. But she nodded and turned to leave.

Mom didn't allow locks on our doors so when Grandma Ann left the room, I grabbed the chair from my desk and shoved the top of it under the knob. I wasn't sure if it would hold if she actually tried to get in, but it made me feel secure. Flinging myself onto the bed, I tried to process everything my grandmother had just told me. I couldn't believe they'd kept this from me. This huge part of me had been hidden under secrets and lies.

I didn't even know what to think anymore. I already knew my mom was self-absorbed, but I never thought Grandma Ann would betray me. As much as we didn't get along sometimes, she was supposed to be my support person, the one who I went to when Mom was busy. Lies were the last thing I'd expected from my grandmother.

"Sherry!" I heard Grandma Ann's voice through the door.

Was Mom home?

I got up from the bed. Mom was going to hear it from me. I opened the door and peered down the hallway but instead of my mother's face, I spotted Grandma Ann on the phone in the kitchen, her back turned toward me.

"I don't care about your meetings, Sherry. This is much more important and you need to listen! Casey knows!" There was a pause. Grandma Ann had her hand on her hip, and her head dipped forwards. "What do you mean, 'knows about what?'" she lowered her voice. "Casey found out about her twin." Another pause. "The girl showed up at her school. Anyhow, that's not the point. She knows and you need to come home now. She's not taking it very well." A longer pause.

I sneaked back into my room just as I heard Grandma Ann speak into the phone. "I'm worried about her."

I closed the door as quietly as I could, putting the chair back into place in front of the door. I didn't like hearing the worry in my grandmother's voice and even though I wanted answers from my mom, I wasn't sure if I could face her just yet.

Grandma Ann was understanding enough not to push me to come out of my room. She left a tray of food at my door, and after knocking gently and telling me that that my dinner was there if I wanted it, she left me alone. But I had no appetite. Instead of eating, I finished packing for camp the following day and went to bed.

The next morning, I didn't remember any of my dreams but by the chaotic state of my sheets and comforter, I knew they weren't good ones.

I woke up before my alarm and lay in bed, trying to go back to sleep. But that was useless, as I couldn't stop thinking about everything that had happened. I was unable to comprehend the fact that Ali was my sister, my twin sister! The idea had been suggested by my friends but I honestly never thought it possible. I'd never considered that my mother would keep a secret like that from her only daughter.

When my alarm finally went off, I got out of bed, grabbed my clothes for the day and headed to the bathroom to shower. Afterward, I ran into Grandma Ann in the hallway. Her short gray-streaked hair was flat on one side from sleeping. There were thick bags of skin under her eyes. She hadn't slept well either.

"Good morning, Casey," she said.

"Morning," I said and flicked my gaze to my

bedroom. She was blocking my way.

"Will you be joining me for breakfast? I'm making chocolate chip pancakes."

My stomach growled, betraying me. I shrugged. "I guess."

She moved in front of my bedroom door as if she thought I would run for cover as soon as her back was turned. The idea crossed my mind, but I was very hungry. Skipping dinner the night before was taking its toll and the thought of chocolate chip pancakes was making my mouth water.

I sat at the table while Grandma Ann went to the stove, pouring the thick pancake batter into the hot pan.

"Do you want to put the chocolate chips in?" she asked.

"No, you can do it," I said.

After a few seconds, the scent of chocolate filled my nose, and a feeling of warmth flooded my body. Even though I was hungry and I loved her pancakes, I wasn't going to give in as easily as she thought.

Grandma Ann flipped the pancake over and said, "I called your mother last night. She's coming home tomorrow evening. It was the first available flight that she could get."

"That's dumb," I said.

Grandma Ann lifted the pancake up from the pan with a spatula and moved it to a plate. "How so?"

"You should call her back and tell her not to bother. I'll be away at camp."

She placed the plate with the pancake in front of me. "I don't think camp is such a good idea."

I looked up at her. "I'm not missing camp because Mom is a liar. Besides, I don't want to speak with her anyway. I've been looking forward to this trip, and Mom's not going to ruin something else for me."

"Casey, that's not fair—"

I choked out a laugh. "Not fair? Mom lying to me for years is not fair. Let's see how she likes it."

I shoved the plate away from me and got up from the table. I wasn't going to give her the satisfaction of thinking she'd won me over with food.

"Casey," Grandma Ann pleaded.

"I'm not hungry. I'm sure Lucas will eat it."

And with that, I left the room. I shut my door and double checked that I had everything I needed. I thought of the things I'd say if Grandma Ann tried to stop me from going, but when she came to my room a while later, she only asked if she could help me carry my bags to the car.

On the way to school, I looked out the window, my head still spinning with everything that had happened. Having a look-alike was one thing. Now I had a twin, and she was in my class at school. The chances of that occurring were too bizarre for me to fully understand, but I guessed I had to now. It was the truth. I felt for Ali who had questioned her parents many times over the years. Now she would have her answers, and we were going to get through this together.

I wondered if she would be happy knowing that we were twins, or upset that her—and my—mother had given her up instead of me. Would she react the same way I had; angry and confused? Or would she be relieved? My stomach twisted. It shouldn't have been up to me to give her this news, but I had no choice. She deserved to know and it seemed that her adopted parents were not planning on sharing the secret. I took a deep breath, preparing myself for seeing Ali and revealing the truth.

CHAPTER ELEVEN

When we arrived at school, there were already a few students and teachers congregated by two yellow buses on the far end of the parking lot. Grandma Ann drove slowly toward them and I sensed her reluctance to leave me.

What I really needed was space and to escape her and the thought of her lies and betrayal. Going to camp would also be the perfect opportunity to get my head straight before I confronted my mother. I wondered if Ali would want to be there when I spoke with Mom but decided that I'd rather confront her on my own. After all, I was the one she'd been lying to for the past twelve years.

Pulling to a stop, Grandma Ann allowed the car to idle. I removed my seatbelt and put my hand on the door handle just as she spoke.

"Are you sure you want to do this, Casey? Your mother is coming home early, regardless. She wants to be here when you get home."

"Mom's coming home early?" Lucas asked excitedly from the back seat. "Cool!"

I ignored him. "I don't care if she'll be back early. I want to go to camp."

I wasn't usually so rude to my grandmother, but under the circumstances, I felt that I had every right and besides that, I couldn't help myself.

She nodded solemnly.

Getting out of the car, I opened the rear door and grabbed my bags, then closed the door a little harder than I intended. I could see Grandma Ann through the window, her expression sad. I felt bad, but she was as much to blame for this as Mom. Even though Mom asked Grandma Ann to lie, she could have said no. She was the responsible one, and she let me down too. I offered a little wave to her before she started out of the parking lot. Then watched the car pull away before lugging my bags to the bus.

When I got to the first bus, I was directed to stow my gear in the luggage compartment. Miss Halliday marked my name off her list and I climbed aboard. Brie waved to me from her spot in the middle and I slumped down into the seat next to her.

"How exciting is this!" Brie said, bouncing in her seat. "I'm so excited. I can't believe camp is finally here. I've been waiting so long for this day to come."

"Yeah," I said, staring at the seat in front of me.

"You okay?" Brie asked.

"I'm all right."

"Casey," Brie touched my arm, and I avoided her eyes. "What's wrong?"

When I didn't answer, she asked again, "We're best friends! We tell each other everything. So what is it?"

I glanced towards her and sighed. There was no way I could keep my news from her. "You have to promise not to tell anyone," I whispered. "I mean it. Like not even write it in your diary."

"Wow! This sounds good. I promise I won't tell a soul."

Looking tentatively around, she moved closer towards me, to make sure she could hear every word I said.

"Remember when Ali said that she was adopted?"

"Yes."

"Well it got me thinking, and when I said something to Grandma Ann about it, she got really quiet like she knew something. I paused for a moment, and Ali sat waiting impatiently for me to continue. "And then she told me that my Mom actually did have twins when she was young. And me and Ali are those twins!"

"No way!" Brie exclaimed, bouncing up and down in her seat again. "I knew it!"

Her beaming smile showed the delight she felt in guessing our secret. She had known it all along.

"Shh!" I said, grabbing her arms and forcing her to sit still. I looked around the school bus, there were only a few classmates around us, but none of them had turned to see what the fuss was about.

Brie pressed her lips together as her eyes widened. "Sorry," she peeped quietly. "Go on."

"So Grandma Ann phoned Mom to tell her that I knew, and she was going to come home early—"

"Are you going to tell Ali?" Brie interrupted.

I shrugged. "I have to. It stinks being lied to, and I don't want to ever lie to her. We're sisters."

"I can't believe it!" Brie squeaked. "This is the most incredible thing I've ever heard."

I started to feel frustrated. "Keep it down." I wanted to be the one to tell Ali, and I wanted to keep this a secret until I spoke with Mom about everything.

Brie ignored me. "My very best friend in the whole world has a twin sister and didn't even know it."

I pinched her arm. "Brie, I'm beginning to regret telling you."

She laughed and covered her mouth. Then she mimed zipping her mouth and throwing away the key.

I looked out the window, wanting to get to Ali as soon as possible before Brie spilled the beans. I knew how bad it felt to have someone other than my Mom tell me the truth.

The bus filled up quickly and only when it was full, did the teachers start to direct students to the other bus. Ali was one of the last to arrive and was forced to join them. I sat back in my seat, upset about missing the opportunity to talk to her on the way to camp, but decided that I'd make a point of getting her attention when we arrived.

That plan went astray when we got to camp. The second we got off the bus, we were separated into cabin groups and instructed to grab our gear and go there with our assigned teachers. I spotted Ali in front of the other bus collecting her bags, but by the time I managed to get my own gear together, she'd already headed off with another group. I couldn't understand how we'd been thrown together every single day at school and then when I really needed to talk to her we had to be separated!

Luckily, Brie and I were in the same cabin. We spent the next hour or so unpacking and organizing our things. I had to keep an eye on Brie to make sure she didn't keep talking about the twins scenario. I'd be mortified if someone else overheard and got to Ali quicker than I could.

A little later, we were all instructed to assemble outside for some icebreaker activities. The minutes stretched on. There were other groups in the distance and I spotted Ali a few times, but we were confined to our cabin groups so I didn't get any chance to talk to her. Even during lunch, Ali was surrounded by other kids and I felt as though the opportunity I needed would never arrive.

After more activities in the afternoon, we were finally given some free time until dinner and I could have jumped for joy. Leaving Brie with the other girls in our cabin, I rushed out the door in search of Ali but there were so many kids around, I never thought I'd find her.

I'd just about given up when I suddenly spotted her sitting on the top step of a nearby cabin. Racing in her direction, I saw a couple of girls filter out of the cabin holding bags and towels. They said something to Ali, and she smiled at them but shook her head. Watching for a second longer, I made sure no one else was around before approaching her. At last it was the perfect opportunity, and I strode up to the cabin, stopping at the bottom of the steps.

"Hey," I said.

"Hey!" she said in return, her gaze flicking to mine.

"What are you up to?" I asked, suddenly feeling very shy. Filled with a nervous anxiety, I wasn't sure exactly what I would say or even if I was doing the right thing. But she needed to know. After all, she was my twin.

"Nothing much," she smiled in her friendly manner. Do you want to sit here for a bit?"

"Sure," I replied, taking a deep breath.

"How was your day?" I continued, making small talk. After thinking about this opportunity for the whole day, I was at a complete loss for what to say.

"It was fun. The girls in my cabin are really nice."

I pointed at a beaded bracelet that she had tied around her ankle. "Did you make that?"

She smiled. "Yeah, in the craft activity. Didn't you make one?" she asked, glancing at my bare wrists and ankles.

"Yeah, I did," I explained, "But I made it too tight and when I tried to loosen it, it broke," I continued. "All the beads fell off and it's in pieces in my bag."

"I could help you fix it?" she suggested.

I waved my hand and shook my head as if to say, "no big deal". We were quiet for a second, and I decided I couldn't hold it in any longer.

"I know this is random, but I need to tell you something."

"Okay."

I hesitated for a second, but then the words came tumbling out and once I started, there was no stopping. "After the sleepover, I asked my grandma if it was possible that my mom had given birth to twins."

I gauged her reaction before continuing. Ali sat stock still, waiting for me to go on.

Taking another deep breath, I answered her unspoken question. "Grandma said yes."

Ali took a deep breath of her own but said nothing.

I stared directly at her, and she stared straight back, listening intently as the words poured from my mouth. "I didn't think it was possible, but I guess she was very young when she got pregnant. She couldn't afford one baby, never mind two, so she was supposed to give us up to two different families since no one wanted twins. But she couldn't go through with it and decided to give up one...

that was you…and she kept me. I haven't had a chance to talk to her yet, but I was so mad when I found out. I'm so sorry Ali. I wanted to tell you right away, but this is the first chance I've had!"

Stopping to take a breath, I watched Ali's expression change. Rather than a look of shock or dismay, her eyes were sparkling with excitement.

It was certainly not the reaction I'd expected.

CHAPTER TWELVE

Ali

I shook my head, trying to calm the racing thoughts. "I knew it," I said, firmly.

Casey's eyebrows furrowed together. "You knew what?"

A fluttering sensation settled in my stomach. "From the moment that I met you I had a feeling, deep down, we were connected. I can't really explain it but ever since the party, after seeing the two of us side by side in the mirror and then finding out we have the same birthdays, it's all I've thought about. To be honest, I was kind of avoiding you today." I wrung my hands in my lap. "I didn't want to freak you out."

"No way!" Casey exclaimed. "OMG! That is such a relief, I've felt just the same."

Nodding in agreement, I explained my own story. "I tried talking to my parents about you, but I didn't want to upset them. I've been going with them to the hospital every day for Mom's treatment. That's why I was late this morning. My dad and I took Mom to the hospital and then he dropped me off at school before going back." I took a breath. "She hasn't been reacting well to the treatment. She seems to be worse rather than better. And I didn't want to bring up the issue of meeting you. Even though I was sure that you must be my twin sister."

"Ali," Casey said, placing a hand on my shoulder. "I'm so sorry. It could have been either one of us who was adopted, it was just the way it happened, I guess."

"It's okay," I said, trying to reassure her. "And besides, I love my parents…I mean, my adopted parents, they mean the world to me. The best news is that we've found each other!"

Casey nodded quietly, as she listened to me speak. "After Ronnie's party, I did some online research about twins being separated at birth. And do you know that there's heaps of cases worldwide? It's crazy!"

"Wow!" Casey replied, raising her eyebrows and her expression becoming more curious. "I didn't know that!"

I explained further, "Well from what I found, if separated twins are lucky enough to reunite, it's usually later in life after the parents finally tell them the truth."

Casey's mouth dropped open a little, as she realized that our situation was not so unique after all.

"And that's what would have happened to us if we hadn't just found each other." I added. "Even if it was by accident, I'm sure it was meant to be. You and I were destined to meet."

Tears welled in Casey's eyes as she wrapped her arms around my neck and pulled me to her. I clasped my hands around her back and squeezed. Her breathing was ragged in my ear, and I felt a tear slip down my own cheek.

"I can't believe this!" Casey whispered. "I have a sister."

"I know!" I said, pulling gently away and wiping my face. "And not just any kind of sister, a twin sister!"

We both began to cry, it was something neither of us could prevent.

"I've always wanted a sister," Casey said. "Maybe somehow, I knew you were out there, and that's why I kept hoping you'd appear in my life."

"Anything is possible," I replied, as I considered the impossible situation before me.

Noticing the girls from my cabin coming back from the showers, I glanced briefly towards them. Casey followed my gaze and moved a few inches away from me. This wasn't a conversation I wanted to share with the rest of my classmates, at least not yet. That was something I'd have to discuss with Casey first. I just hoped they didn't notice our red eyes and the obvious fact that we'd both been crying.

The girls walked up the steps, immersed in their own conversation and barely taking note of us. We waited until they were inside the cabin before we faced each other again.

"We should meet after dinner and lights out," I suggested. "So we can talk more."

"Good idea," Casey agreed eagerly. "But I don't think we should share this with anyone yet. Do you mind keeping it secret? But I'm sorry, I have to admit I've already told Brie."

"That's fine," I said. "She's your best friend. And I really like her."

Casey bit her lip. "She only knows part of it. I think we should keep some of it to ourselves."

I nodded. "Whatever you think is best."

Casey let out a sharp breath. "Okay." She stood up, and we hugged again, quicker this time. "I'll see you after dinner and lights out."

"See you soon," I said.

Watching as Casey walked away, I couldn't help the excitement from bubbling inside me.

CHAPTER THIRTEEN

Casey

I made my way back to my cabin to get ready for dinner. Brie was there, laying on her bed reading a book when I arrived.

I sat on the edge of her mattress. "Hey."

She looked over at me and sat up right away. "I was wondering where you went off to. Did you talk to Ali?"

"Yeah."

"Spill!"

She beamed with excitement, desperate to hear my news.

I quickly pressed a finger to my lips, turning around to see if anyone else was listening. The other girls glanced over at us but soon returned to their own conversations.

Lowering my voice, I explained the details. "I told her about what Grandma Ann said. And do you know, she wasn't even that surprised? She said she knew it all along. But her mother did tell her she was adopted so I guess it made sense that we could be sisters and separated at birth."

I didn't tell Brie about the weird psychic connection between Ali and me. The entire situation was already strange. Brie knew enough, I wanted something to remain a secret. At least for now. Discovering that I had a real twin sister was freaky enough, I certainly wasn't sure that Brie would believe the psychic thing. I wasn't sure that I believed it myself.

"This is major," Brie said. "What are you going to do next?"

I shrugged. "I guess I'll wait until we get back home so I can talk to my mom about it all. I was so angry with her but now I'm not sure how I feel. I'm hoping Ali comes along too so we can confront her together. Can you imagine her reaction? That'll be payback for keeping it from us for so long. And besides, I'm sure Ali has a lot of questions. I know that I certainly do!"

Right then, I could barely wait for dinner to be over so Ali and I would have a chance to talk some more. As it turned out though, that never happened. There were several teachers patrolling the area and keeping an eye on everyone. Although, I tried several times to escape from my cabin unseen, I didn't find a chance. I just hoped that Ali wasn't waiting in the dark for me to arrive. Somehow though, I felt sure she'd know I wasn't coming.

When I finally climbed into my sleeping bag that night, I pushed the curtain aside and stared out the window in the direction of her cabin. Only a short distance away I had a real-life twin; a girl who looked just like me. As I closed my eyes, I pictured her face, my face, and I knew that right then, she was thinking the exact same thoughts as my own.

To our huge delight, the following day my cabin group happened to be paired up with Ali's for the activities for the entire day. I wondered whether it was luck or fate that had intervened. Whichever it was, I didn't really care, I was just grateful that it had worked out the way it had.

Immediately, I rushed to Ali's side, at the same time giving Brie an apologetic smile. But I knew I could rely on my best friend, who had already urged me to pair up with my sister. Brie was more than happy to pair up with Holly so it all worked out well.

Since confiding in each other the day before, my connection with Ali seemed stronger than ever, and my previous dislike was a thing of the past. In its place was the feeling that I was right where I was meant to be.

The first activity was archery. I'd had no idea that Mr. Pavoni was practically an expert at archery. He showed us how to properly hold the bow and where to place the arrow. This time, I was not upset when he paired me with Ali. It allowed us to spend even more time with each other, and out in the open, rather than in secret.

Mr. Pavoni did a double-take this time after making the pairing. Though he didn't say anything, he'd finally caught on that we looked alike!

Ali and I glanced at each other and smiled.

As it was her turn to try first, she held the bow the way Mr. Pavoni instructed, with one eye closed and focused on the target. She bit her lip in concentration, and let go. The arrow bounced on the ground a few feet in front of us.

She sighed and looked at me. We laughed.

Handing me the bow and still laughing, she asked. "Do you think you can do better?"

I took the bow from her and lifted an arrow from the bunch. "Probably not."

Moving my body into the correct stance, I placed the arrow on my finger. I took a deep breath and noticed I was biting my own lip in concentration. Smiling to myself, I recognized yet another trait that Ali and I shared. I let go of the arrow, and it flew straight towards the target. The arrow dropped a few feet from the target but it was still further than Ali's attempt.

"Alright," she said. "Gimme that. I want to try again."

I handed her the bow. Our fingers touched, and I could have sworn I felt an electric zing between our fingers. If Ali felt it, she didn't let on. Maybe my connection to her was stronger? Though when our eyes met, a certain spark lit her eyes. She did feel our connection. I knew it. I felt it deep down inside of me. She didn't have to say anything at all. I wondered what else would come up the more time we spent together.

On the way to the next activity, Ali and I laughed over the hilarious misses we'd made in archery. Mr. Pavoni said we'd have another session before camp ended, and I decided that I would try harder next time. There was a friendly rivalry between the two of us, and I was excited give it another go.

"The way your arrow flew right over the top of the target!" Ali said, shaking her head.

"Hey," I said. "At least it reached the target!"

We both burst into a fit of laughter.

"What's so funny?" Brie asked.

I didn't realize she was beside me. "Brie, you had to be there," I scoffed grinning widely.

"Oh," she said, a little hurt.

Noticing her reaction, I felt bad and made sure to include her. "It's just that we missed the target every time. We were both pretty hopeless."

"Yeah, I saw that," Brie laughed, feeling proud of her own attempts, which I'd noticed were much more successful than my own.

"You're good at archery, Brie!" I grinned back, giving her a quick hug. She was my best friend and I reminded myself not to forget that. I'd hate to hurt her feelings, that was something she did not deserve.

With the three of us laughing over our archery attempts, we headed up the steps to the recreational building where tables were set up with a multitude of objects. Breathing a sigh of relief, I realized we weren't making more beaded bracelets. I didn't want to embarrass myself again with my poor tying skills.

"Key chains," Ali said, recognizing the activity. "Cool."

Once everyone settled down, the teacher, whose name was Miss Tucker confirmed Ali's guess. "Once you have assembled your keychain, raise your hand, and I will come over and help you with securing it."

When she was finished, we went to work. Immediately, Ali and I reached for the same pink keyring. The table was filled with a huge variety and we could have chosen any of them, but instead, we targeted the same one. Glancing instinctively at each other, we laughed.

"This might sound strange," Ali said in a small voice. "But do you feel, like, odd around me sometimes? Not in a bad way, but—I don't know what I'm trying to say."

"Yes," I responded.

Her eyes widened. "I thought I was the only one?"

"No," I replied, smiling. "You're not." It was a relief to hear her say that. It was the one part of our friendship that neither of us had really discussed.

"What are you two whispering about?" Brie asked, leaning across the table to grab a piece of leather.

"Nothing," Ali and I stated at the same time.

"Are you two still doing that?" Lacey chuckled. "You're like clones."

"Close," I said under my breath.

Ali grinned, and I met Brie's eyes winking at her.

She smiled.

It was our secret and I knew it was safe with Brie.

CHAPTER FOURTEEN

Lunch break was next and then everyone was to take part in a ropes course. We had about ten minutes before having to be at our designated places, when Ali abruptly turned to me with a proposition.

"You know what would be really fun?" she whispered quietly so no one would hear her.

"What?" I asked, finishing my glass of chocolate flavored milk. Wiping the excess from my lip with a napkin, I waited curiously for her to continue.

"When I was looking for information on identical twins, I found a heap of stories where some switched places and in many cases, their friends and family didn't even realize."

I looked around to make sure no one had been listening, but everyone was talking loudly and focused on their own conversations.

"You want to trade places?" I asked, raising my eyebrows curiously.

She shrugged and her smile widened. "Just until dinner. Don't you think it'd be fun?"

I chewed my lip. "I'm not sure." My cheeks flushed at the idea of playing a trick on my friends and teachers. What if it didn't work? And what if we were caught out? I'd hate for us to be sent home from camp.

"Come on," Ali pleaded. "If it doesn't work then it doesn't work. We should try, though. This is the perfect opportunity. And it'll be fun!"

I took a breath, deciding to accept the challenge. "Alright. But only until dinner."

"Yes!" Ali said, pumping her fist in the air. "Okay, let's clear our plates, then head to the bathroom."

Following quickly behind her, we made our way into a cubicle each and passed our clothes under the wall to each other. When we emerged, we both stared into the mirror, laughing.

"Whoa," I said, unable to take my eyes off myself. Ali's clothes fit perfectly, and I imagined myself being her. I smoothed my hands over her soft shirt. Ali's clothes were a lot nicer than mine. Maybe this swap-thing wouldn't be so bad.

Ali reached for my hair.

"What're you doing?" I asked.

She looked at me in the mirror. "My braid is the only thing that sets us apart. Here, let me do it for you before we leave."

I watched the transformation take place as Ali expertly braided my hair.

Her fingers moved quickly down the strands until the braid was complete. She loosened her own braid and let the waves fall over her shoulders the way mine always did.

We checked ourselves over one more time before we heard the teachers telling our classmates to file outside.

"Ready?" Ali asked.

"Ready!" I said, high fiving her, before making my way to the door. My hands shook with anticipation of what we were about to do but at the same time, I felt a thrill work its way down my spine.

"Oh! And don't tell Brie," Ali said. "I want to see how long we can trick everyone for. If we can fool her, we can fool anyone!"

I hated lying to my best friend, but it was only a little prank. We played tricks on each other all the time, this was no different. Right?

"Deal," I replied with a smile, before stepping a little hesitantly out the bathroom door.

Convinced that we'd be caught right away, I felt my cheeks flush red, but no seemed to be taking much notice of us at all. Miss Halliday beckoned for us to keep moving and we made our way towards the throng that was already lining up outside.

"Let's go, ladies," Miss Halliday said.

"She has no idea," Ali said, confirming my thoughts.

I giggled into my hand. "This might actually work."

"I told you!" Ali exclaimed and beamed widely.

We were one of the last to arrive at the ropes course and headed towards Brie and the other girls.

"Here we go," Ali said.

I nodded and was about to take my place by Brie's side when Ali moved in front of me. Duh. That made sense. She was pretending to be me. I had to act like Ali now. I wasn't sure what that entailed. I wished we'd had a little time to prepare being each other.

"I'm so not ready for this," Brie said to Ali.

"I'm sure you'll be okay. This looks fun," Ali said to her confidently.

Brie snorted. "Easy for you to say, you actually like all

of this athletic stuff. You always have."

Ali glanced over her shoulder and shot me a grin. Even Brie was falling for this! I had to contain myself.

After safety instructions had been given, we were split into groups. Ali—as me—went off to the lower course while I was grouped with Brie and a few others for the higher course.

"Have you ever done something like this before?" Brie asked.

I almost remarked that I'd tried it at camp the year before, but held my tongue just in time. Tugging on the end of the braid that draped across my shoulder, I reminded myself that I was playing Ali, not Casey.

"No, I'm a little nervous," I replied instead, hoping that was something Ali would say.

A breath whooshed out of Brie. "Me too! I'm glad I'm not the only one."

Stumbling a little at first over how to respond, once I concentrated and channeled what I knew of Ali's personality, I fell into a rhythm that was both exciting and a little scary. I couldn't believe not one person guessed that we'd swapped. Not even my best friend had any idea it was me who was right beside her. And wondering how Ali was doing, I caught a glimpse of her a few times on the other side of the course. It really was striking to see me from across the way. But it appeared that she had taken to the transformation as well as I had.

From the high ropes course, we were directed straight to the dining hall and Ali and I decided to continue the charade during dinner. Sitting next to each other, it was easier to keep up the ruse as we fed off each other's comments. And being so close to her I could channel her inner thoughts much more easily. I didn't question the psychic connection we appeared to have. It had come out of nowhere and was unnerving at first, but already it seemed like second nature.

Excusing ourselves to the bathroom mid-way through the meal, we rushed to swap clothes, and we also wanted some privacy so we could talk.

"I can't believe it worked!" I said, laughing and in awe, the moment we were alone.

"I know!" Ali said from the next stall as she handed my shirt and shorts under the divider, and I did the same.

"Even Brie had no idea," I said. "She spoke to me as though I were you - she had no idea that we'd actually been friends for years!"

"I told you we'd get away with it," Ali replied cheerily and I could hear the smile in her voice.

After changing back into our own clothes, Ali braided her hair again, and I smoothed my own hair into long strands over my shoulders and moved my pink head band back into place.

Locking eyes in the mirror, Ali spoke, "I think we could do this again!"

I could not mistake the mischievous grin on her face.

"Yes, let's do it!" I agreed eagerly. If no one noticed today, then I doubt they would any other time."

An idea suddenly formed in my head, but I wondered

if I should say it aloud. Glancing at Ali who was concentrating on braiding her hair, I decided that after everything we'd discovered, it would be silly to keep something from her.

Blurting out the words, I could feel my cheeks flush a little with embarrassment. "Do you like Jake?" I asked.

Ali shrugged. "I guess. He's been nice to me."

She continued braiding and then a moment later, she picked up on my meaning. "Do *you* like Jake?"

I cleared my throat. "Kind of."

Ali jumped up and down. "We have to do this again! Then you can talk to Jake, and pretend to be me. Maybe that'll help your shyness around him."

"I'm not shy—"

"You are around him!" Ali laughed "I've seen the way you behave. I don't know why I didn't put it together before."

I chewed on my lip, wanting to be certain before continuing with the idea. "Are you sure you don't like Jake that way? I mean it's obvious he likes you!"

I'd just discovered I had a twin and did not want to jeopardize our relationship, especially over a boy.

Ali sighed. "There's too much going on to think about boys. With my mom's illness and all. Besides, you liked him first. What kind of sister would I be if I got in the way?"

I smiled. "Okay, if you're sure about Jake, let's swap again tomorrow."

The excitement was working its way through me and

already I could hardly wait for the following day to arrive.

"After breakfast," Ali agreed. "Let's meet in here and swap clothes again."

I nodded happily, following Ali to the door. As I watched her walk away, I wondered how I would ever get any sleep that night. My stomach fluttered with anticipation over Jake. I knew I had to pretend to be Ali, but it meant I got to spend time with him and it was certainly a start.

I could hardly wait for the next day to arrive.

CHAPTER FIFTEEN

As the weather forecast predicted clear blue skies with a blazing sun, water activities had been scheduled for the day. I was a little nervous about the canoeing activity. We weren't going on any wild rapids, but it still made my stomach turn to think about it. Sometimes I became queasy in boats, even on still water, and I would be mortified if I embarrassed myself in front of my classmates. And since I'd promised Ali we would swap places for the day, I didn't want to embarrass her either.

I didn't mention my nervousness when we swapped clothes and hairstyles in the bathroom that morning. She might change her mind and I really wanted Jake to notice me for a change, rather than being the onlooker, as was usually the case.

"Are you okay?" Ali asked.

"Yeah," I said a little breathless. I was glad for the divider between us so she couldn't see my face. "I didn't sleep much last night." I feigned a yawn.

"Me neither," she replied. "The girls in my cabin do not stop talking."

"Have you ever been canoeing?" I continued.

She snorted. "Casey, if I haven't been to a sleepover or a camp before, do you think I've been canoeing?"

"Maybe your Dad is outdoorsy?" I said with a smile. I

fed off Ali's excitement for the swap.

Ali's stall door opened. "No way. He's more of an indoorsy-type.

I adjusted the fit of Ali's two-piece bathing suit on my body, taking in the beautiful shimmering shade of blue and how lovely it looked against my skin, before lifting her shirt over the top. It was the latest style and I could hardly wait to show it off.

The hair swap had become a part of the routine too. Mom used to braid my hair when I was little, and I'd never had my hair braided since. Thinking of my mother reminded me of the shock she would feel when she eventually saw the two of us together. I could only imagine her reaction.

"Ready?" Ali asked as she finished the braid. I broke away from thoughts of my mom when I noticed the birth mark on her shoulder. I'd completely forgotten about it when I chose a sleeveless tank top to wear that day, but it was too late to go back to my cabin for a different one. "Remember to hide the birthmark. Keep your hair over it so it's covered. It's the only way anyone can tell us apart."

She glanced down nodding, too caught up in the excitement of what we were doing to allow her birth mark to be an issue. "Let's do this."

After breakfast was over, we made our way down to the river. Several of our teachers were already waiting by the canoes. Mr. Pavoni stepped forward and held his hands in the air, signaling for us to stop talking.

"There will be two people per boat," he said. "We're splitting the classes into boy-girl pairs so find yourself a partner."

I turned to see Jake heading right for me. I flushed when his eyes locked with mine.

"Hey Ali," he said.

My insides deflated. Of course, he thought I was Ali, but for a split second, I almost wished he would have partnered up with the actual Ali since she was playing me. I only hesitated for a second before smiling at him. At least it would give me some time with him and maybe after he got to know me a little more, he'd eventually want to hang out with the real me. It was all very confusing, but I wasn't about to pass up the chance to be his partner, especially in our own little boat.

"Hi," I said.

"Want to be partners?" he asked.

"Sure!" I said a little too quickly and enthusiastically.

If my reaction was weird, Jake didn't show it. Instead, he grinned at me. "Cool."

I turned to find Ali who was partnered with Jordan Lockwood. He was in another class and I wondered how that had happened because it was likely that he didn't really know her. I wondered if she'd chosen him or it was he who had picked her.

With no time to worry about the Ali - Jordan issue, I followed Jake towards the pile of life jackets where he immediately offered to find me one. Passing it to me, he grabbed one for himself and then indicated a nearby canoe.

"I think we should take that one," he said, pointing to one that had a red stripe across it. "Red is my lucky color."

I smiled. "Sounds good to me."

Standing by our boat, I realized that Jake was close enough that I could smell his minty toothpaste. He was concentrating on the instructions being given and I risked a glance towards him, taking in the fall of his long dark hair across his forehead. I then found myself wanting to brush it out of his eyes, at the same time wondering what it felt like to touch. When he suddenly turned towards me, I felt my cheeks flush and looked quickly away, hoping that he hadn't noticed me staring. That would have been so embarrassing.

With my stomach churning nervously at the thought of Jake as my rowing partner, my anxiety abruptly worsened when he maneuvered the canoe to the middle of the river. But before long, we'd fallen into a steady rhythm of rowing together and I began to relax a little.

He sat in the back behind me and I pictured his handsome face in my mind.

But all the while I tried to think of something to say.

Usually, I was chatty and outgoing, but around Jake, I was a different person. To my relief though, his constant chatter soon put me more at ease. "You're a pretty good rower," he commented from behind me.

Taking a quick glance around, I grinned, "I'm just doing my best not to capsize us." I wasn't sure if it was the calm water of the river or Jake's easy-going personality but I felt myself relax even further.

He laughed in response and I felt my insides flutter. My smile turned to a wide grin at the sound of his voice behind me. "Don't worry, I'll make sure we don't capsize."

"How do you know so much about this?" I asked.

"My parents love to go camping. We have a couple of canoes and we often take them out. It's such a fun sport. My dad and I usually use the canoes to go fishing."

"I always wanted to learn how to fish."

"Your Dad never taught you?" he asked.

I almost admitted that I didn't know anything about my dad, but caught myself just in time. I had to remember that I was Ali, and her father was present in her life. But with Jake so close, it was hard to concentrate.

"No, not yet," I replied, turning slightly towards him.

"I can teach you sometime," he said. "It's casting that's the trickiest. Apart from that, there's nothing to it."

Glancing over my shoulder, I smiled. "That'd be great."

"Cool."

"Cool," I repeated quietly to myself, finding it difficult to believe that I was really in a little boat on a river with Jake .... as my partner.

But then I remembered that he thought I was Ali and some of the thrill disappeared. I wanted him to like me, Casey, not the girl who was my twin. I wondered how he'd react to know that I'd tricked him. But then I considered the idea of not telling him what we'd done. If I built up enough confidence, perhaps I could approach him on my own. Ali had made it clear she wasn't interested, so maybe his interest in her would switch to me when he realized how well we got along.

It was all so complicated! But I decided to shake off the worry and enjoy my time with Jake. I'd just have to figure out the rest later.

We canoed for the next hour and I became more comfortable as the time went by. Even when Jake pretended to capsize the boat, swaying it from side to side, my squeals turned to fits of laughter. Then when he really did tip the boat over and we were both tossed into the cold water, I gasped when I came up for air. Splashing him, I pretended I was annoyed but then he splashed me back and the game was on. When he turned the boat back over and climbed back in, he reached down to help me up. I was sure that the day could not get any better!

During lunch, I filled Ali in on my morning.

"I was watching you guys," she said. "You and Jake were having so much fun! I knew this swap was a good idea."

"How did you do with Jordan?"

Ali smiled. "Not so well, but it was fun trying."

I happened to look up at the same time Jake was staring at me from the next table. He gave me a little wave and my whole body flushed.

"Wow, he really likes you," Ali said, noticing him too. "He can't stop looking this way."

"I know, right? It's so strange."

Ali and I giggled together which caused a few looks from the girls at the table. Brie's eyebrows were raised. Her eyes darted between us.

I didn't want to ruin the game, so I stopped laughing and continued eating my grilled cheese.

On the way to free swim time, I confided in Ali about Jake. "You know, at first I was really jealous of you getting along so well with him."

Ali's eyes widened. "Oh no! I told you I don't like him like that."

"I know," I said. "But I didn't know that at the time. It was pretty annoying that he never gave me any attention and then you arrived, my absolute look-alike, and he could not take his eyes off you."

Ali shook her head, denying that it was true. But I knew it had been the case and I wasn't the only one who'd noticed.

Clearly there was something about Ali that attracted people to her. Even Jordan Lockwood, from a completely different class, had rushed to be her partner for canoeing.

But rather than feeling jealous, as I would previously have done, I felt grateful that she was so willing to help me. I smiled appreciatively at her as I thanked her again for swapping identities.

Draping an arm around my shoulders, she replied, "Anything for my sister."

The temperature had spiked that afternoon and all of my classmates, except for a select few who sat under the shade of the trees, were in the water. The teachers had set up a floating volleyball net, and there was a rope lane for races. Ali, Brie and I found a spot away from the activities, happy enough to enjoy swimming on our own.

"Let's see how long we can float on our backs!" Brie suggested.

We flung our bodies back and allowed the slow current to move us over the surface of the river. My mind drifted to the morning and how much fun I'd had with Jake. I didn't realize how long I'd been floating until Miss Halliday's frantic voice called out.

"Ali!" Miss Halliday called. "You're drifting away, swim back to shore please."

I looked over my shoulder at Ali who was closer to the shore than I was. She had a confused look on her face. I followed her gaze and realized Miss Halliday was looking at me!

I dipped my legs into the water, and waved to my teacher, signaling that I'd heard her. I swam closer to Ali, noticing her bare shoulders.

"Casey," I whispered pointedly.

Ali turned to me with a smile.

"Your birthmark," I said in a voice just above a whisper.

She lowered herself under the surface until only her neck and head were visible. "Thanks," she said.

Thankfully Brie hadn't noticed our exchange.

"Hey Ali," Jake said as he swam past us, a friendly smile on his tanned face.

Ali poked me in the side under the surface of the water.

"Hi, Jake," I said, smiling.

He made a point of splashing water at me, before swimming away again,

I looked at the girls. Brie was staring at Ali. I knew that she was waiting for "Casey" to react. And I could see the surprise register on her face when she saw Ali's wide grin and nod of encouragement. Clearly, she was quite confused as to why "Casey" would be acting that way, when Jake was showing such obvious interest in "Ali."

With an effort to distract her, I splashed Brie with a handful of water and suggested we race each other to the shore. Then, without waiting for a response, I began to swim, fully aware that she would not be able to resist a challenge. Sure enough, she fell into pace beside me, and raced me to the shore.

Quickly I grabbed our towels and threw mine to Ali who immediately wrapped it around her shoulders. It had taken no effort whatsoever for her to pick up on my meaning and once again, I was grateful for our psychic connection.

Unfortunately, it began to rain during dinner, so the campfire planned that evening was postponed until the following night. Instead, we were given permission to hang out in the recreational building where there was a ping pong table, a pool table, several comfy couches and a variety of board games. Ali, Brie, Lacey and I played checkers.

"I'm so thirsty!" Lacey said, getting up. "Anyone want water?"

When we all nodded in response, Brie offered to help. "I'm going to grab more cookies too. I'll go with you."

The girls left and Ali and I sat quietly alongside each other, Ali yawning widely.

"I'm not looking forward to going to the cabin tonight," she moaned.

"Why not?" I asked curiously. It was the first time I'd heard her complain about anything.

"The girls in my cabin talk all night about boys and makeup. It was okay for the first night, but I can't sleep when there's so much noise."

Out of nowhere, I was struck with a brilliant idea. "Why don't you sleep in my cabin tonight? The girls in my cabin all want sleep, so no one stays awake very late. As soon as it's lights out, that's pretty much it for us. And no one will notice you're not me."

"Oh, that's okay," Ali said chuckling. "We've probably done enough swapping for one day."

"Ali, I'm serious," I insisted. "Why not? If you're tired, then take advantage. It won't bother me, I can sleep through anything."

"Really?" Ali sat upright in her seat, the idea obviously catching her interest.

I nodded. "My mom used to tell me how surprised she was that I could sleep through Lucas's crying when he was a baby. Trust me. I'll be fine. You look exhausted."

She hesitated, staring quietly towards me and I could almost hear her brain ticking over with the idea.

"Besides, your decision to swap places gave me a chance to hang out with Jake. It's the least I can do."

"Alright, if you're sure it's ok?" she asked once more.

"Yes, absolutely," I smiled at her reassuringly.

A breath whooshed out of her. "That will be amazing! Thanks so much, Casey."

"What are sister's for?" I asked with a smile.

CHAPTER SIXTEEN

Ali

The last hour of downtime went by quickly. Although I hadn't admitted it, I was a little nervous about sleeping in Casey's cabin, but as Casey reminded me, if no one noticed throughout the entire day that we'd swapped places, then it was highly unlikely that anyone would notice when we were sleeping.

When I followed Brie inside, I stayed close by her. Casey had said her bed was next to Brie's. She also explained where she'd put her clothes and toiletries. As the cabin layouts were all the same, it was easy for me to figure out where everything was. I didn't intend to use her toothbrush, but a little toothpaste on my finger was better than nothing and I did like to brush my hair before bed. I was sure she wouldn't mind if I borrowed her hairbrush.

One of the girls, Amanda, who for some strange reason had decided to dye her hair green for camp, seemed to be in charge when it came to the sleep schedule.

"Five minutes, girls," she said, clapping her hands. She sounded like a teacher, but I was looking forward to getting into bed so I didn't mind her bossy attitude.

The weight of sleep began to press on my eyelids. I changed into a set of pajamas from Casey's designated drawer and sat on her bed. But my usual habit of brushing my hair to one side had been a terrible mistake.

Brie let out a little gasp, and I glanced up at her.

She bolted over to my bed and sat next to me, pointing at my exposed shoulder and my birthmark.

I quickly covered it with my hair.

Brie's eyes darted around the room before they settled on mine. "Ali?" she asked in a low voice.

"Shh," I said.

"Where's Casey?" she asked.

"In my cabin. She said I could sleep here tonight since the girls in my cabin are so loud. They just don't sleep!"

Brie shook her head vigorously. "But—but—how long have you been pretending to be Casey?"

I swallowed. Casey trusted Brie but I'd been caught out. I just wasn't sure how Brie would feel about Casey keeping this from her. I'd hate for Brie to alert the other girls to our game. If the teachers found out what we'd been up to there was no way of knowing how they'd react.

"Most of yesterday and all of today." I stared guiltily at Brie, holding my breath anxiously.

Brie clapped her hands over her mouth.

"Don't say anything," I begged.

Brie looked a little hurt. "How come neither of you told me?"

"We wanted to see how long it would take anyone to notice. And then Casey started talking to Jake and—"

Brie snapped her fingers. "They were hanging out all day! I wondered why Casey—or you—didn't mention it. She told you about her crush right?"

I nodded.

Brie shook her head, dumbfounded. "And they were hanging out all day! She must be so excited!"

I smiled. "She is."

"Whoa," Brie said. "I should be upset that you two kept this from me, but I'm so happy for Casey."

"Me too. But, Brie, you must keep our secret. I'm not sure if we're going to swap again tomorrow, but if we do, you can't tell anybody at all."

Casey had already mentioned that Brie could keep a secret, but sometimes in her excitement, she let details slip. I was careful not to say anything about my mom around her. I didn't need anyone to feel bad for me.

"I cross my heart," Brie said, making an imaginary 'X' over her chest.

Amanda clapped her hands again and then she flipped the light switch by the door. The room was abruptly shrouded in darkness. I blinked a few times, letting my eyes adjust to the sudden change.

Brie squeezed my arm. "Good night. Hope you sleep well, *Casey*."

Her over-accentuation of Casey's name was a little obvious, but I let it go. My body craved sleep, so I snuggled under the covers of Casey's bed and closed my eyes, falling quickly into a deep coma.

CHAPTER SEVENTEEN

Casey

The next morning, I was the first one to wake and at first I was disoriented. But after clearing the sleep from my head, I remembered I was in Ali's cabin. Ali had been right about her cabin-mates. I'd managed to drift in and out of sleep but I was sure they'd been chatting and giggling for most of the night. I ignored most of it, except for their gossip over the boys in our grade which did catch my interest, especially when Jake's name was mentioned. A girl called Ashleigh went on and on about how cute he was. It sounded to me that she had a crush on him herself.

"He's so cute!" I heard her gush. "Don't you think he's the best-looking boy in our grade?"

They all took turns at guessing who he liked. That was until one of the girls, I couldn't tell who, shushed the others and mentioned Ali by name. They assumed she—meaning me—was asleep but didn't want "her" to wake up and hear them talking about Jake.

I smiled against my pillow. It had been obvious to everyone that Jake preferred Ali and possibly liked her, well me. It was all so confusing. Maybe it would be best if I told him outright that he'd been hanging out with me instead of Ali. At least we could start our friendship off properly, and he'd see that he really preferred me over her. I was sure Ali wouldn't mind, she didn't like him that way anyway.

I was already showered and dressed before any of the girls woke up and I left the cabin ahead of them, making my way towards the dining hall for breakfast.

On my way, I caught sight of Ali and Brie who'd obviously got up early as well and I hurried to catch up.

"Hey, Ali!" Brie said. "Decided not to braid your hair today?" She looked at me with a grin and I caught the cheeky expression on her face.

Shoot! I didn't realize that I got ready this morning as Casey, leaving my hair down. "Oh, uh. Yeah, I decided not to."

"I told her," Ali said, in a matter of fact voice. "She found out, so I had no choice!"

I looked innocently from one girl to the other, pretending I didn't know what they were talking about.

"Oh come on!" Brie said laughing. "Admit I had you there for a second."

I grinned back at her as she explained how she'd found out. I'd always known that Brie would be the hardest one to fool but if it hadn't been for Ali's birth mark, I was sure there was no way she could have known.

Then I realized that Brie had a point, "Should I braid my hair?" I asked Ali.

She shook her head. "No. I'm beginning to like it down too. I bet no one will be able to tell us apart."

I played with the hem of Ali's shirt. I was sure people would be able to tell right away who was pretending to be whom. Ali's clothes were much nicer than mine. But I didn't say anything.

Ali had been right, though. As the kids came into the cafeteria and passed our table, most did a double-take.

My heart thudded in my chest when Jake put his tray down at our table and slid into the seat next to mine.

"Is anyone sitting here?" he asked.

"N-no," I stammered.

"Cool," he said.

"Morning, Jake," Ali said.

My eyes widened, and I looked at her. There was something in her expression that told me to keep my mouth shut.

"Hi, Casey," he said.

Brie kicked me under the table, and I gave her a tiny shrug.

"Did you like canoeing yesterday?" Ali asked him.

"I love canoeing." He picked up a piece of toast from his plate and started eating.

"Me too!" Ali said excitedly.

"Really?" Jake said.

"Yes, I love outdoorsy things."

My breathing quickened, and I started to understand what she was doing. Ali's natural outgoing attitude was helping me get an "in" with Jake. She was pretending to be me, starting the conversation with Jake and then when we switched back I wouldn't have to be so nervous. At least that's what I thought she was doing. It was hard to tell sometimes with Ali. At times, I felt we shared one brain, which was ridiculous but entirely possible considering we were twins.

"Me too," he said.

His gaze darted between Ali and me. "You know, I always thought you two looked alike, but today you look like twins."

"Everyone says that," Ali said.

"I'd say it was a compliment," I added.

Ali smiled at me, and we all continued eating. Ali chatted some more with Jake and each time he replied, I felt butterflies fluttering crazily in my stomach. This whole camp had been a dream come true and I'd almost forgotten what I would be going home to in a few days. Deciding to push that though from my head for the time being, I focused on enjoying the time I had left.

We had a few minutes left before breakfast ended when Ali and I excused ourselves from the table. I had an idea, and I wasn't sure if Ali would go for it, but there was no harm in asking.

After we'd swapped back into our own clothes, I outlined the plan.

"You want to swap houses too?" Ali asked, as we stood in front of the mirrors. Whether it was pure habit or because of the hot steamy air outside, I wasn't sure, but she began to braid her hair.

"Don't you want to meet your real mom?" I asked.

Ali considered this.

As much as I wanted to know more from Mom about giving up one of her kids, I was still angry with her. And it would be perfect payback for her to face the child she had given up for adoption. I didn't say this to Ali. Once Ali was at my house, I'd make a point of visiting and then Mom would have to face the two of us. I wasn't sure Ali would agree to the second part of the plan, so I had to have her in the house already when I arrived. Then Mom would feel awful for what she had done. As much as I loved the idea of having a twin sister, I wasn't ready to forgive my mother just yet, for the years of lies.

I smiled, imagining the shocked expression on my mother's face.

"I don't know," Ali said.

The bathroom door burst open, and a few girls entered. Ali and I moved just outside the door so we could keep talking in secret.

"Why not?" I asked.

Ali finished her braid, wrapping a hair tie around the

end a few times. "I don't want to upset my mom if she finds out we did this. Her condition is getting worse, and I think this would hurt her."

"She won't find out," I said. "I promise. How about we only do it for one night? And I can keep you updated on her as much as you want."

Ali sighed. "I really do want to meet my birth mom…"

I let her think about the plan for a few seconds while my insides twisted with anticipation.

"Alright, I'll do it," she answered, suddenly coming to a decision. "One night couldn't hurt."

Jumping up and down with excitement, I threw my arms around her in a quick hug. "That's so awesome!"

Ali grinned. "I finally get to meet my real mom. Wow! I can't believe it!"

"It will be great," I said, pumping her up. Everything was falling into place. And both of us would get what we wanted.

"And let's keep this to ourselves," I added. "Except for Brie. She likes to be included, and I trust her to keep this secret."

"Deal," she said.

"Oh! Thanks for talking to Jake as me," I said.

Ali smiled and draped her arm over my shoulder. "Anything for my sister."

I smiled back. I loved having a twin.

As the camp grounds were soaked from the drenching of overnight rain, we did indoor activities all day. I crossed my fingers that we'd still be able to have a campfire that night. All day I formulated a plan with Ali that would put Jake and me together. My hopes were high as a few times he approached me to talk about whichever activity we were doing.

I imagined Jake and me sitting together, making s'mores by the fire...it was going to be a perfect night.

Usually, my imagination took me away to experiences I knew deep down would never happen. But miraculously, the campfire plan worked! I almost jumped for joy when Miss Halliday announced that the campfire was still on.

Ali, Brie and I arrived early, looking for the perfect seats. The bonfire was lit and the fire was raging.

"Is this too close?" I asked, checking out the other kids arriving and searching for Jake in the crowd.

"It's fine," Brie said. "Look, there he is."

I swatted her hand, hoping he didn't see her pointing towards him. Her enthusiasm was going to mess everything up.

Jake was with his cabin-mates. He looked so good in his black skinny jeans and light blue t-shirt. And without even thinking about it, I caught his attention and waved him over.

Surprised at myself, I felt nervous butterflies fluttering crazily inside me. Calling him over was something I would never have even considered before, but it was my chance to talk with him as myself instead of Ali doing all the work for me.

"I saved you guys a seat," I said, indicating the spaces beside me.

He and Jordan sat down, and the other guys in his group scattered, sitting in other unoccupied seats.

"Thanks!" Jake grinned, and I noticed the pleased expression on his face. "This is a good spot.

My cheeks flushed as I smiled back, and the butterflies in my stomach continued their crazy dance.

Feeling a little awkward at first, I was soon grateful for Brie's excited chatter, it helped so much to have a chatty person in the group and before long all of us were talking non-stop about our day. A couple of times I caught Jake smiling at Ali, and I had to control the small twinge of jealousy that I felt inside. Ali however, made a point of taking little notice and before long most of his attention was directed towards me.

By that time, I was so much more at ease with him and able to relax and just be myself. The two of us even had a s'more eating contest, which he won by two whole s'mores. Laughing at his efforts to fit in his fourth s'more, I clutched my own stomach which was already so full. The heat from the fire had become quite hot and a few of the others had moved away, but I didn't dare budge from my spot beside him. We were getting on so well and there was no way I wanted to leave his side. I also noticed that when his friends moved away, he continued to stay alongside me.

When we were eventually sent back to our cabins to prepare for bed, Ali grabbed hold of my arm and whispered in my ear, asking if we could swap for one more night. She wanted to make the most of the opportunity to practice switching identities, especially if we were planning to swap houses.

I agreed that it was probably a good idea and as I was so happy about the Jake situation, I would have agreed to anything right then. I watched as Ali raced ahead so she could reach the cabin before the other girls and change into my pajamas.

But even though I had to pretend I was Ali again, inside I was soaring! Jake wanted to be near me all night. Me! Not Ali. And I felt as though all my dreams had come true.

I made my own way back to Ali's cabin, grabbed the bathroom before anyone else and then climbed into bed, not bothered at all by the light still shining brightly and the non-stop chatter of the other girls. When Molly, the girl who slept in the bunk above Ali's bed, asked me what I thought about Jake, I smiled awkwardly and tried to brush the question away. But I could not help the red flush that crept onto my cheeks and I knew it was a dead give-away.

Molly laughed, commenting on how cute she thought Jake was and each of the others agreed. They assumed it had been Ali sitting with Jake at the campfire all night and found it hard to believe that the new girl already had the hottest boy in the grade interested in her. Shaking my head with embarrassment, I could not help my wide grin. Then, to escape any more questions, I yawned and rolled over pretending to go to sleep. I just wanted to be alone with my thoughts and the image of Jake's beautiful smile in my head.

The girl's voices were a distant sound that I pushed away as I focused on visions of the campfire with Jake alongside me.

CHAPTER EIGHTEEN

The next morning, I woke up to the sound of the other girls frantically rushing around the room, complaining that they'd overslept again and were going to be late for breakfast. I blinked open my eyes, the edges of my sight blurry. My head ached, and when I got up from the bed, I realized I was in a lather of sweat and my pajamas were sticking to my body.

I told the girls not to wait for me. I wasn't at all hungry and asked them to tell Casey and Brie that I'd meet them at the stables after breakfast. Our groups were scheduled to do horseback riding that morning and it was going to be the highlight of the whole camp.

I made my way to the bathroom to get showered and dressed. But I could feel my legs giving way beneath me and fumbled my way back to the bed. Suddenly everything went black.

The next thing I knew, Miss Halliday was sitting on the bed alongside me. I glanced at her worried expression as she placed her hand gently on my forehead,

"Ali, you're burning up!" Her brow was wrinkled in concern. She offered me a glass of water, but I could only manage a small sip.

"It looks like you have a nasty fever," she said, as she placed a cool cloth on top of my forehead. "I'm not sure that you're well enough to stay."

Sitting up abruptly, the cloth fell onto the bed as I

shook my head weakly. "No, I'll be fine, honest. Maybe I can just skip this morning's activity and get a little more sleep. I'm sure I'll feel much better in a little while."

The last thing I wanted to do was go home and miss out on the rest of camp, especially when I'd finally become friends with Jake. I could not let them send me home.

Then another thought struck me. Right then, she thought I was Ali, so there was no way I could have her sending me anywhere. My head was throbbing and I could feel the flush of my skin. I felt hot all over and just wanted to sleep.

Trying my hardest to convince Miss Halliday, I gave her a small smile and tried to reassure her that after a short rest, I would be fine.

Shaking her head reluctantly, she stood to leave.

"Okay, Ali. I'll just be down on the grass with the archery groups. You'll be able to see us from your cabin door. If you need anything, just call out. I'll keep coming back to check on you, but if you don't improve, I'll have to your parents."

And with that, she was gone. But by then, my head was in such a thick fog that I could do nothing but close my eyes. All I wanted was sleep and within seconds, I drifted off.

CHAPTER NINETEEN

Ali

After breakfast, our group was instructed to line up at the stables for horseback riding. I looked around for Casey, who had still not appeared and I wondered what was taking her so long. I was so excited. It was another first-time experience for me, and I simply couldn't wait! When I glanced towards the horses lined up waiting, I hoped to be given the beautiful white one that stood quietly at the end of the row. Once again, Casey's group and mine had been placed together for this activity, which was a perfect opportunity to talk more about our house swap.

When the instructors arrived, and asked us to gather closer, I looked around for Casey once more.

"Casey still hasn't shown up," I whispered in Brie's ear and she glanced around worriedly.

"I don't know where she could be!" Brie exclaimed. "She was really looking forward to this activity, I can't believe she'd miss it!"

Making my way to Mr. Pavoni who was our supervising teacher that morning, I pointed out to him the fact that Casey still hadn't arrived.

"Miss Halliday just called me," he said quietly in my ear, not wanting to interrupt the instructor's spiel as she explained what we would all be doing.

"Apparently, Ali is unwell and she's resting in her cabin," he continued. "Hopefully she'll feel better later and can join in with a different group tomorrow."

Frowning with disappointment, I looked up the hill towards the cabins, and thought of Ali in bed on her own. It was so unfair that she had to get sick. I just hoped that she'd be okay. Then when we were asked to line up for a riding helmet, I was forced to shake thoughts of Casey away as I concentrated on all the instructions being given.

The pony I ended up being paired with was a chocolate brown horse named Trina. And as soon as I was asked to lead her around the enclosed arena, I found that she was very quiet and very obedient, perfect for a beginner rider such as me.

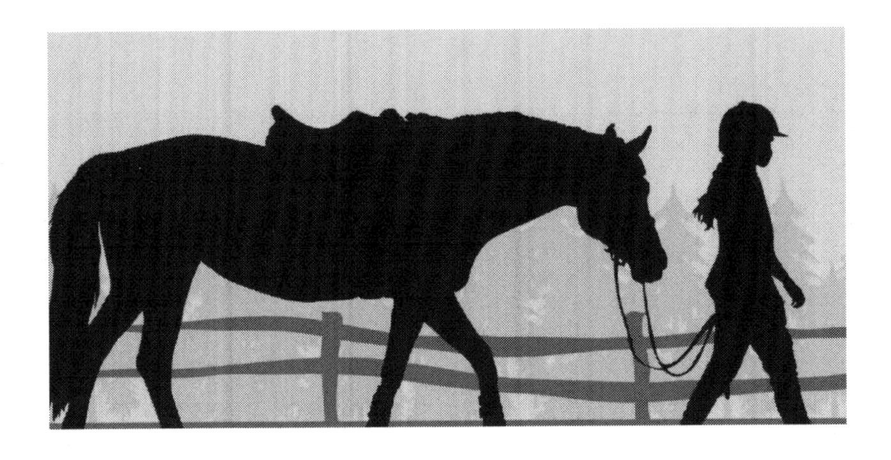

When I later realized that the beautiful white horse was much friskier and less obedient, I felt relieved that I'd been given Trina to ride. She did exactly as I asked, even if it was the wrong command. But try as I might, my mind was not fully focused on riding. My thoughts kept wandering to Casey hoping that she was okay. For some reason, I felt a constant niggling inside that something was not right and I could not help but worry.

After almost an hour into the ride, I began to lose interest, my focus still on Casey. We had another half-hour to go, but all my thoughts were directed towards my twin. The minutes dragged on, and when we finally got back to the stables, I jumped off Trina, tied her to some timber fencing as instructed, and headed in the direction of the cabins.

"Al—Casey!" Brie called.

I turned to her and gave her a look. She'd nearly given us away by calling me the wrong name.

Brie jogged over to me. "We have to help put the gear away and clean the stables."

"Really?" I asked, my frustration worsening. All I wanted to do was check on Casey.

Brie shrugged. "It's more than just a horse ride. We have to learn responsibility or whatever. We do it every year. I know you're worried about Casey, but we have to do this. Casey's probably still asleep. I'll go with you afterwards and we can check on her."

I sighed heavily, glancing back towards the cabins, but with no other option, I was forced to follow Brie and try to get the work done as quickly as possible. My anxiety over Casey was getting worse, and I could not control it. Eventually, my hands were practically shaking with the anticipation of seeing her again.

Finally, we were finished and Mr. Pavoni told us we had fifteen minutes before lunch to go and change if we wanted to. I was desperate to get to the cabins. More specifically, my cabin.

With Brie at my side, I could feel the throb of my pulse quicken as I raced up the hill. Something was wrong. I had no idea what, but I felt my concern worsen with each step. The top of the hill was so close yet so far. The muscles in my legs burned. If I stopped, I would probably fall over and not reach the top. I pushed through the uncomfortable cramps in my legs and abruptly stopped at the top of the steep incline. I leaned over, catching my breath. Then, as I glanced up, my worst fears were realized and all I could do was stand and stare.

The familiar car pulled out of the lot. The girl in the backseat turned her head. She had the exact same profile as me. Where was she going? Why was she leaving? And now what was I supposed to do without her?

"Ali?" Brie asked. "What's wrong?"

I shook my head, unable to believe what I was witnessing. "Everything!" I exclaimed. "That was my parent's car, I'm sure of it."

Brie stared at me with a confused expression. "It could be one that looks like your parents' car. Why would they be here?"

My stomach dropped.

Miss Halliday's voice floated up from the other side of the hill. I rushed over to her. She was informing the others that we had a short amount of time before lunch.

"Miss Halliday!" I said, rushing over to her.

"Yes, Casey?"

I cringed at my sister's name. Why did we ever play

this silly game?

"There was a large yellow car here. It was driving past the cabins and I could see a girl in the back."

Miss Halliday pressed her lips together in a thin line. "I'm sorry Casey. I know you and Ali were getting close. She was too ill to stay at camp. I had to call her parents to come and pick her up."

Brie grabbed my arm and squeezed.

Miss Halliday turned to speak with another teacher.

I turned to Brie, speechless and in shock.

Brie's face abruptly filled with comprehension. "Did she—?"

I nodded. "Casey was in that car!"

***

Find out what happens next in Twins 2.

Available NOW!

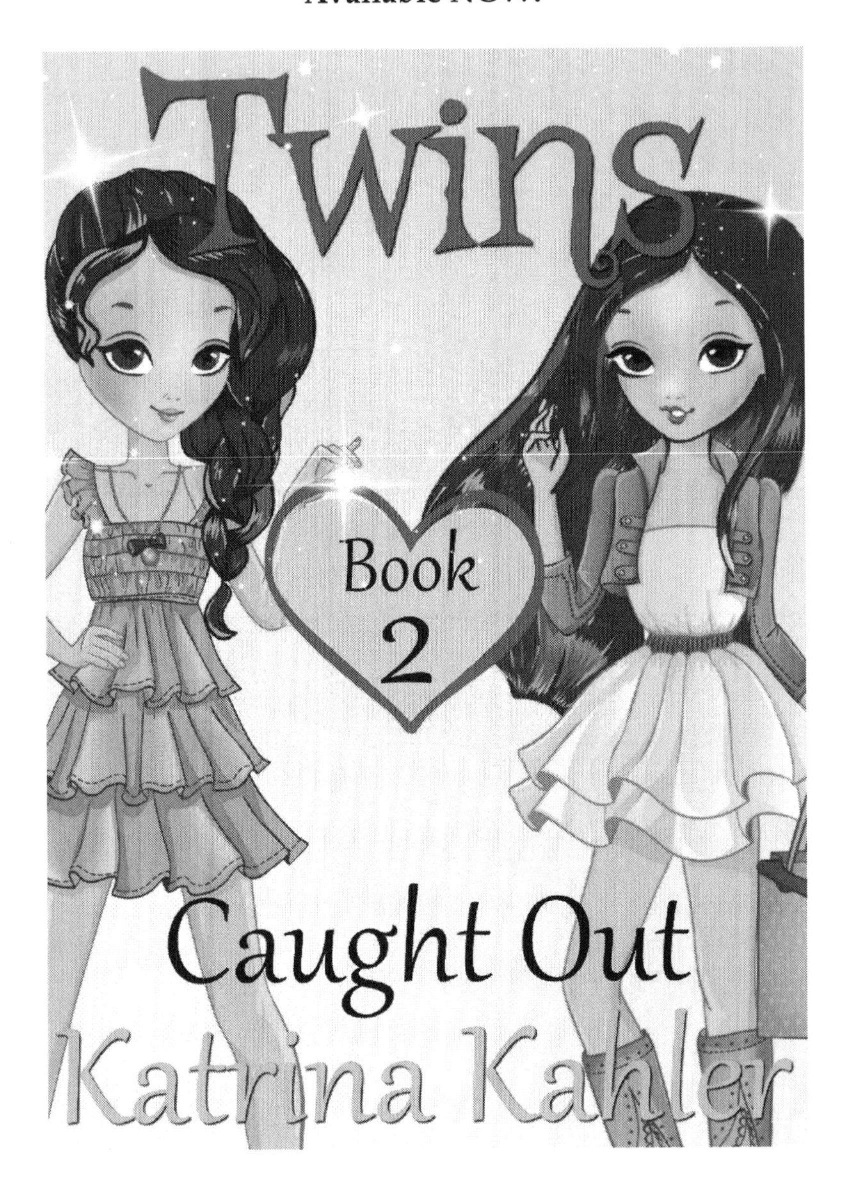

Follow us on Instagram @juliajonesdiary

And please LIKE Julia Jones' Facebook page to be kept up to date with all the latest books in every Katrina Kahler series…

https://www.facebook.com/JuliaJonesDiary

***

Thank you so much for reading Twins.

If you could leave a review, that would greatly help me to continue to write more books.

Thank you so much!!!!!

Katrina xx

Some more books you may like:

MIND READER
BOOK 1
MY NEW LIFE
KATRINA KAHLER

THE SECRET
MIND FREAK
BOOK 1

Body Swap
Catastrophe
ZAP!
Book 1
Katrina Kahler

Witch School
Book 1
Katrina Kahler

49581524R00075

Made in the USA
San Bernardino, CA
29 May 2017